A Willowdale, Indiana Story

A Dog's Life

A Novel

Carla J. Underwood

M u d P i e s P r e s s
FOUNTAIN HILLS, ARIZONA

Carla J. Underwood/Mud Pies Press
13235 N. Verde River Dr., #308
Fountain Hills, Arizona 85268
www.mudpiespress.com
carla@mudpiespress.com

Publisher's Note: This is a work of fiction. Names, characters, places and incidents are a product of the author's imagination. Locales and public names are sometimes used for atmospheric purposes. Any resemblance to actual people, living or dead, or to businesses, companies, events, institutions, or locales is completely coincidental.

Cover Design © 2017 by Dawn Underwood
Book Layout © 2014 BookDesignTemplates.com
Cover Layout © 2014 BookDesignTemplates.com

A Dog's Life/Carla J. Underwood--1st edition
ISBN 978-0-9978780-3-5

To all the pugs in my life-
Kalvin, Maya, Priscilla, Sassy, Spot, Ug Lee

Preface

What can be said about a family pet? To a casual observer, it might appear to be just another animal. To a devoted pet owner, it is a member of the family—an integral part of daily life.

A perfect example of a devoted owner is Aunt Maude. The close bond between her and her little pug is unshakeable. But George is also Willowdale's unofficial mascot. His well-being is the concern of most of the residents of the small town.

All the farms surrounding Willowdale have at least one large dog. Unlike George, most of them are trained to be guard dogs against intruders and predators. Not pets.

Pugs, on the other hand, are bred for one purpose. That is to be companions to their owners—to love and to be loved. In that role George excels.

Table of Contents

Preface 5

One 9

Two..17

Three..21

Four 23

Five..29

Six..37

Seven 41

Eight 47

Nine 55

Ten..61

Eleven...67

Twelve...73

Thirteen 79

Fourteen..89

Fifteen...95

Sixteen...99

Seventeen..105

Eighteen..109

Nineteen..115

Twenty...123

Twenty-one..127

Twenty-two 133

Twenty-three 143

Twenty-four 153

Twenty-five... 157

Twenty-six 163

Twenty-seven.. 169

Twenty-eight 177

Twenty-nine 181

Thirty... 187

Thirty-one 193

Thirty-two 199

Thirty-three 205

Thirty-four.. 209

Thirty-five 215

Thirty-six.. 219

Thirty-seven 225

Thirty-eight 233

Thirty-nine 243

Forty.. 249

Forty-one.. 253

Forty-two.. 263

Forty-three.. 269

About the Author 279

One

"You stupid truck."

I slapped the dashboard twice, but not because I thought it would help. I was frustrated and tired.

Since Grandma's handyman's eyesight was too bad to drive anymore, I was in charge of running errands. Unfortunately, the truck wasn't any friendlier to me than it was to Mr. Martin.

When I tried to shift gears, they rewarded me with a loud grinding noise. After that, they refused to shift at all.

"Maybe Grandpa was right," I said to myself. "Maybe girls shouldn't drive."

No, that wasn't right. All my girlfriends and I were licensed, and all of us were pretty good drivers.

I dismissed Grandpa's old-fashioned idea and tried a trick Pastor Lawrence once said might help. Since he was the one who taught me to drive, I trusted his advice.

I pressed the clutch pedal twice and tried changing gears again. That didn't work. The truck was stuck in neutral, and I was stranded in Mrs. Van Berkel's driveway.

"Sorry, Grandpa," I said, looking upward. "I just can't get your truck to work."

Of course, Grandpa couldn't hear me. He had been gone for two years, but I talked to myself a lot.

I started talking to myself when I was a little girl. Mom worked full-time after Dad passed away, and I spent a lot of time alone. I figured it was okay to talk to myself if nobody was there to hear me.

"Listen," I said to the stubborn gearshift. "I can't take all day."

Grandma was waiting for me at her café. She had no patience for tardiness, and I didn't want her mad at me. I had to get the eggs to her cook before the breakfast crowd arrived.

"How can Irene cook breakfast without eggs?"

I tried to shift gears one more time, but the lever refused to budge. My first day as Grandma's driver looked grimmer by the minute.

"Please, Grandma, don't give up on me."

I gave the dashboard another slap and tried to shift gears one last time. Hard as I tried, the lever refused to move out of neutral.

"Looks like I'm walking back to town."

I eyed the six cartons on the seat next to me. I remembered how hot and tired I had been on egg day last summer. The last thing I wanted to do was walk to town again with cartons balanced in my arms.

I turned off the engine, grabbed the key from the ignition and jumped out of the cab. I fought the urge to give the old truck a big kick.

"Don't worry, Grandpa," I said, looking up again. "I won't do that."

I walked around to the passenger side and opened the door. As I started to gather the cartons, a truck rounded a curve on the graveled road. It threw up a cloud of dust behind it.

It was Jim Spencer in his father's truck, waving at me out the driver's window. I hadn't seen him since last August, and I couldn't wait to catch up on the news. As the truck got closer, I saw he wasn't alone.

"Uh–oh."

I expected to see Aunt Maude's pug, George, on the seat with him, but he wasn't. Instead, there was some girl I'd never seen before.

Jim pulled into Mrs. Van Berkel's driveway and stopped the truck next to me. He flashed his usual wide, toothy smile.

"Hey, Shirley."

"Hi, Jim."

I had a clear view of his passenger sitting on the other side of the cab. I disliked her immediately.

She didn't say a word, but she didn't have to. Seeing her next to Jim caused my unreasonable teenage jealousy to ooze to the surface.

"Well, Jim," I said. "How are you?"

I hoped I sounded casual. As if my being stranded with Grandpa's 1939 Chevrolet truck was an everyday occurrence. I didn't want him to know how hurt I was that he was with another girl.

"I'm good," he said.

"That's nice."

"Just get to town?"

"Last night."

"Welcome back."

"Thanks."

That was awkward, and I didn't know why. We were just friends, but seeing him with another girl turned my brain to mush.

"On your way back to the café?" he said.

"I was—sort of."

"What do you mean?"

The stranger with strawberry blond hair and blue eyes looked back and forth between Jim and me. She still didn't speak. I wondered if there was something wrong with her.

"Grandpa's truck isn't cooperating," I said.

"It's a good thing we happened to be driving out this way, isn't it?"

I looked through his window and scanned the interior of the cab. All I saw was the girl and a picnic basket on the seat. No George. Obviously, his "we" didn't include the little pug.

"Where's George?" I said.

Before Jim could answer, my unreasonable teenage jealousy was replaced by my unreasonable teenage temper. Unable to stop myself, I jammed my fists on my hips and started rambling.

"You promised Aunt Maude you'd take good care of him," I said. "All I see is you two driving around and having a picnic or something."

Jim's mouth dropped open, and I forced myself to wait for an answer. That girl was sitting where the little pug was supposed to be. I wanted to know what was going on.

"Take it easy," he said, holding up his hands as if he were surrendering.

"Well?"

"George is good."

"Oh, yeah?" I said, my right toe tapping up and down. "Where is he?"

I probably looked and sounded a little crazy, but I didn't care. Aunt Maude counted on Jim and me to keep her sweet little dog safe. I wanted Jim to know I took that responsibility seriously.

"What's the matter with you?" he said, dropping his hands to the steering wheel. "He's at the mill with Dad."

"Hmm, and who is she?"

I couldn't stop myself. I sounded like a crotchety old woman, and it wasn't a pretty picture. It was especially ugly considering I was only sixteen.

"This is Betty," he said. "She's here for the summer, too."

"Hi, Betty," I said, leaning down and resting my arms against the truck's door. "Where are you from?"

I wasn't the tiniest bit interested, but I thought I should at least be polite. After all, it wasn't her fault I was jealous of her and angry with Jim.

"Bowling Green," she said.

She turned away from me and tilted her chin upward. Her voice was as beautiful as her face, but it was cold and flat.

"Is that the one in Ohio?"

"No," she said without looking at me. "Kentucky, of course."

Before I could say anything more, Jim nudged his door open. I dropped my arms and stepped back, giving him just enough space to get out.

"What's wrong with your truck?" he said.

"How should I know?"

He slid his baseball cap from his head and slapped it against his pant leg. Dust and chaff flew everywhere. I was surprised to see he had cut his curly blond hair.

"A crew cut, huh?"

"Yeah," he said. "Betty likes it better this way."

I wanted to remark about his new hairstyle, but I didn't get the chance. He put his cap back on and nodded at the cartons in Grandpa's truck.

"Your grandma needs those eggs, right?"

"Yeah, so?"

"If you want help," he said, "you have to give me a clue about what's wrong."

I didn't want to look helpless in front of the girl, but I needed his help. The eggs needed to be delivered, and carrying them a mile to town wasn't my preferred option.

"The gears are stuck," I said.

"Let me give it a try."

I handed him the key. He walked around Grandpa's truck, climbed into the cab and started the engine. After fiddling with the gearshift, he didn't have any better luck than I did.

"Yep," he said. "It's stuck."

I already told him that, but I forced myself to keep quiet. If he could teach me how to get it unstuck, I'd never need his help again.

Two

"Ye gods and littles fishes, where is my granddaughter?"

Marie Ivey paced in front of the café's front window and studied the customers waiting outside. Some of them sat on the new wooden bench in front of the window. Others gathered along the walk, shielded from the June sun by the green canvas awning.

"No sign of her yet?"

Irene thrust her head through the kitchen service window. As usual, her blond hair was pulled back into a single braid. Her bib apron, secured tightly around her ample body, was stained with fresh bacon grease.

"I told Shirley to be back half an hour ago," Marie said. "What could possibly be keeping her?"

"She'd never be late if there wasn't a problem," Irene said.

At the mere suggestion of trouble, Marie accelerated her pacing. The faster she walked, the more floor area she covered.

"You don't suppose somethin' really is wrong, do you, Marie?"

She stopped her pacing and glanced over at her cook. She placed both of her hands over her heart and took several deep breaths.

"She did have difficulty last summer getting the pastor's car stuck on that old bridge."

"Oh, Marie, I upset you, didn't I?"

"Shirley is my responsibility while she's in Willowdale," she said. "I never gave a thought to an emergency."

"She'll be just fine," Irene said. "She's a smart girl—like her grandma."

Marie dropped her hands to her sides and began pacing again. Thinking about Shirley in trouble made her more agitated as the minutes ticked away.

"I was afraid she was no longer the responsible young woman she was last summer," she said. "I can't imagine all the terrible possibilities."

Irene came out of the kitchen and walked to the front of the dining room. She wiped her hands on her apron and looked at the crowd outside.

"There's lots of folks out there," she said.

Marie stopped pacing to check the clock on the wall above the magazine rack. In five minutes, she would have to unlock the front door and let her customers inside.

"What could be wrong?" she said, pacing again. "All she had to do was drive to Mrs. Van Berkel's farm and buy some eggs."

"Pacin' won't get her here any faster," Irene said. "It sure as shootin' won't solve the egg problem."

Irene shook her head, and her braid wagged back and forth. Several of the customers had their faces up to the glass, staring at her.

"You can't keep those folks waitin' forever."

Marie stopped pacing. She was worried about her grand-daughter, but the success of her café was her immediate concern.

"I have never opened the café late, Irene," she said. "I have no intension of doing so today."

"What about the eggs?"

Marie glanced at the front table where her late husband's favorite chair still stood. She imagined him there, working on the café's ledger and imparting his quiet wisdom.

After he passed away, the café became her responsibility. It was up to her to make all the decisions in its operation.

"What can you make with the eggs you have now, Irene?"

The cook pulled her braid around in front of her and grabbed the end. She twisted it between her fingers.

"I can make lots of pancakes, I guess."

"That's what you do," she said. "Go back to the kitchen and make a lot of pancake batter."

"How much do you reckon we'll need?"

"As much as it takes," Marie said. "Now, let's not worry about the eggs and make this a special occasion."

"How do we do that?"

"I have just decided," Marie said. "We make today the first annual Ivey's Café Pancake Day."

Irene tossed her braid behind her back. A somewhat tooth-less smile lit up her face. She clapped her hands and let out a hearty laugh.

"Good idea," she said. "Your Robert would get a real kick out of that."

"He would indeed, wouldn't he?"

On her way back to the kitchen, Irene stopped at the blackboard menu on the wall. She took the eraser from under the counter and wiped away the bacon and eggs special. With a piece of chalk, she wrote "Pancake Day".

"There," she said. "It's official."

Marie nodded in approval and waited until the cook was back inside the kitchen. When she thought Irene could no longer overhear her, she faced Robert's chair at the front table.

"Irene is right, Robert," she said. "You would definitely get a kick out of this."

Solving the latest crisis didn't make her worry any less about Shirley. What grandmother could stop worrying about her grandchild?

At that moment, however, her obligation was to her customers. They depended upon the café operating as usual.

"Please be alright, Shirley," she said. "Please be alright."

Marie stood up straight and brushed out a wrinkle in her bib apron. She tucked a loose strand of hair into the bun at her neck and hurried to the door.

Just as the wall clock chimed seven times, she turned the key in the lock. One at a time, the customers filed in, and she greeted each one by name.

Three

It was only a few minutes after opening, and the dining room was already crowded. Marie busied herself between pancake orders by refilling coffee cups.

"If that don't beat all," someone said.

She was at the back table when she heard the voice over the rest of the conversations. She looked over at the lunch counter at her usual group of breakfast customers.

"Did you say something, Horace?" she said.

He stopped eating his pancakes and wiped his mouth on the sleeve of his shirt. He dropped his fork on his plate and pointed at the front window.

"Yeah, Mrs. Ivey," he said. "You gotta see this."

He poked his elbow into the side of the man sitting next to him. Like a chain reaction, everyone at the counter stopped eating.

Marie hurried to the front of the room. When she looked out the window, she stopped short. What she saw caught her by surprise, and she nearly lost her grip on the carafe.

Jimmy Spencer and his new girlfriend were sitting in the cab of his father's truck. They were stopped in the middle of the street directly in front of the café.

Robert's old truck was attached to its trailer hitch by a rope, and Shirley was behind the wheel. She looked angrier than Marie had ever seen her.

"Why's Jimmy towing Mr. Ivey's truck?" one of the other farmers said.

"Precisely," Marie said. "Why, indeed?"

As if on cue, everyone in the dining room stood up and rushed to the window. They completely blocked Marie's view.

Not to be outdone, she shoved her way through the line of customers. With the carafe still in her hand, she pushed the front door open and rushed outside.

"Ye gods, Jimmy," she said. "What is the meaning of all this?"

"Hey, Mrs. Ivey," he said. "How's it going?"

Four

It was only my first day as Grandma's driver, and I already broke Grandpa's truck. I didn't think the day could get any worse, but I was wrong.

Jim had tried to get Grandpa's truck in gear. When he couldn't manage that, he decided to tow me to town.

We borrowed a frayed rope from Mrs. Van Berkel and tied it between the two trucks. Since she didn't want the rope back, I decided I'd store it in Grandpa's truck.

"Now, remember," I said to Jim. "Take me straight to the garage so Grandma doesn't see us."

"Don't worry," he said. "She'll never see a thing."

Instead of stopping at the garage, he towed me and Grandpa's truck right to the front of the café. What part of sneaking into town didn't he understand?

Since I was tethered to his truck, I was at his mercy. I had no choice but to stop when he stopped.

I looked over at the café and moaned. There was a crowd standing at the front window, staring at me. I could feel my face turn red from embarrassment.

"Where did all those people come from?" I said to myself. "Besides that, why is Grandma standing on the sidewalk with a carafe in her hand?"

Being towed back to town by Jim would have been fun if it hadn't been for Betty. She constantly stared at me through his truck's rear window. I felt humiliated and angry at the same time.

"Oh, Grandma," I said to myself. "What must you think of me now?"

Jim turned off his truck's engine and twisted around in his seat. Leaning halfway out the driver's window, he looked back and shouted at me.

"How're you doing back there, Shirley?"

I was too mad at him to speak. I gripped the steering wheel tighter and looked up at the wooden water tower behind the café.

The lettering on its side was still bright red. Just the way Jim and I painted it last summer before I left for home.

"At least Jim and I did that right."

It wasn't the time to pat myself on the back for a beautiful paint job. I still had to deal with being late for work.

"Shirley?"

Without stopping to check for oncoming traffic, Grandma rushed over to Grandpa's truck. I didn't know why she was carrying the carafe. I was pretty sure it wasn't to serve me some coffee.

"Well, young lady," she said. "It seems you have a problem."

"I'm sorry I'm late, Grandma," I said. "I have the eggs right here."

I motioned to the cartons next to me and gathered them into three stacks. I picked up one of the stacks and reached for the door handle.

"I'll get these to Irene right now so she can start cooking breakfast."

"There's no need to rush," she said. "Irene has Pancake Day completely under control."

"Pancake Day?"

Before Grandma could explain, Jim and Betty appeared out of nowhere and stood beside her. I couldn't imagine what they were doing.

"Here," Jim said. "Give me those."

I gladly handed him the two cartons I was holding. I reached across the seat for two more.

"I suppose I could take a couple of those, too," Betty said.

I was surprised she offered to help, but I didn't waste any time wondering about it. I handed her the two cartons and grabbed the last two for myself.

Grandma stepped back, and I eased out of the truck. The three of us lined up behind her and followed her into the café.

Thankfully, her customers were sitting down again and eating their breakfasts. They didn't look up from their food or even speak to us. That was fine with me.

Not stopping to talk to any of her customers, Grandma marched us through the dining room. She only paused long enough in the kitchen to set the carafe on the stove.

Irene was busy ladling batter onto the griddle and flipping pancakes. She didn't seem to notice us. We walked right past her and followed Grandma to the walk-in cooler.

She took one carton at a time and arranged each one on the shelf next to the milk. None of us said a word until she was finished and closed the door.

"I know I'm late for work, Grandma," I said, "but I still have to get Grandpa's truck to the garage."

"I see."

"The gears stuck again, and Jim tried to help."

"I see."

"He couldn't get them to work either, so he towed me back to town."

"Yes, I see that."

I expected her to lecture us about irresponsibility and tardiness, but she didn't. We stood in a line in front of her and waited while she studied our faces.

"It's been quite a morning for all of you, hasn't it?" she said.

"Don't be too hard on Shirley," Jim said. "Gears on an old truck can be really tricky."

"I'm sure she wouldn't have been late if the truck hadn't broken down," Betty said. "Would you, Shirley?"

What did she know about me, and who did she think she was? I didn't need her to defend me to my own grandmother.

Grandma didn't respond to either of them. Instead, she edged past us and walked to the front of the café. We followed along behind her like three little ducklings.

The dining room seemed more crowded than usual, and I didn't recognize anyone seated at the tables. At the lunch counter was the usual assortment of farmers in dirty overalls.

I was surprised to see they weren't eating their normal orders of bacon and eggs. They were eating bacon and stacks of pancakes instead.

"That's weird," I said under my breath.

"Did you say something, dear?"

"Just thinking out loud is all."

Grandma stopped at the front door, and we stopped next to her. I couldn't read the expression on her face, but she sounded almost sad when she spoke.

"I want you three to finish towing Robert's truck," she said.

"Yes, ma'am," Jim said.

"Yes, Grandma."

"Yes, Mrs. Ivey."

"I expect you and Betty to return here for breakfast," she said to Jim. "As my guests."

"Yes, ma'am."

"Yes, Mrs. Ivey."

"Grandma?"

I didn't know why I was surprised by Grandma's invitation. She believed every act of kindness must be repaid with an act of kindness. Offering them free breakfasts was her way of paying Jim for helping me with Grandpa's truck.

She was generous as usual, but there was something different about her I couldn't pinpoint. Her eyes didn't sparkle, and her warm smile was missing. Something was definitely wrong.

"You, young lady," she said, looking directly at me. "You have a great deal of work to do when you return."

"You're not mad at me for being late?"

"Was there anything else you could have done?"

"No."

"If you did your best, there's nothing more for me to say."

I reached over, threw my arms around her neck and gave her a long hug. She didn't return my hug, but I thought I heard her chuckle a little.

"Oh, Grandma," I said. "You're the best."

Five

Jim turned up 1st Street, circled behind the café and drove to the filling station on Main Street. He towed Grandpa's truck and me around the gas pumps and stopped in front of the garage. I coasted to a gentle stop in front of the open service door.

The only other vehicle in sight was a rusty Model T Ford parked next to the building. Thankfully, the mechanic offered to delay the restoration on it long enough to repair Grandpa's truck.

"Thank you, Mr. Graves," I said. "Grandma really needs the truck as soon as possible."

"My daddy's name was Mr. Graves," he said. "Everybody calls me Earl."

In my family, no one my age addressed an adult by his first name. It wasn't easy for me to break that rule, but I didn't want to insult him.

"Thank you,—Earl."

"No problem," he said. "Just leave the keys in the truck."

When I stepped outside, I put the keys above the visor and looked for Jim and Betty. They were in Mr. Spencer's truck, and the rope was coiled in the bed of Grandpa's truck.

I wasn't sure what to do next. Instead of walking over to them to say good-bye, I waved at Jim and turned toward the café.

"Thanks for the tow."

"Sure thing," he said. "See you in a few minutes."

I listened to the rumble of Mr. Spencer's truck behind me as Jim drove away. When he didn't offer me a ride, it became obvious Betty was his first priority.

"I guess beauty wins over brains every time."

Although my feelings were hurt by his snub, I really didn't mind the walk. It gave me time to think about how much Grandma had changed.

She grew a little older, of course, but there was something else different about her. She seemed—sad.

"What is it, Grandma?" I said to myself. "What aren't you telling me?"

When Grandma asked me to spend another summer in Willowdale, she said it might be my last. I assumed she was referring to my senior year in the fall and plans I might have after graduation.

"Is that it, Grandma," I said, "or is there more to it than that?"

Instead of crossing the street, I decided to walk on the opposite side from the café. It was interesting to see Grandma's building from that perspective.

It looked as pristine as ever. Grandma insisted the bricks be cleaned every spring and repointed every few years.

Grandpa used to scrub the awning every summer to keep it looking new. I guessed that became Mr. Martin's job after he passed away.

On the other hand, the empty lot next door was a mess. It was overgrown and weedy, and old pop bottles were scatter around. There were even weathered newspaper pages and other paper scraps caught in the weeds.

"Guess the lot isn't very important to you."

Mom told me Great Grandma and Grandpa Ivey bought the lot a long time ago. She didn't know why they bought it or what they wanted to do with it.

"It looks horrible," I said to myself. "I don't know why I never noticed before."

I wasn't usually on the opposite side of the street looking at it, but that was a poor excuse. I needed to ask Grandma why she didn't have somebody keep it mowed and picked up.

"Okay, Shirley," I said. "Stop daydreaming and get to work."

Instead of crossing the street, I continued up the sidewalk toward the old general store. Some stranger from Monticello bought it after Aunt Maude got sick, but I couldn't imagine a new owner.

As I got closer, the front door swung open and a middle-aged woman stepped outside. She was tall and thin, and her long, strawberry blond hair was streaked with silver. She was beautiful enough to be a model.

I stopped short and stared at her. The resemblance to Betty was uncanny, and I think my mouth was open.

"Good morning," she said. "Are you alright?"

"Huh?"

My mind was racing trying to make sense of the woman. I couldn't get any words to form.

She moved a little closer to me and studied my face. I must have looked strange with my mouth open, so I closed it.

"Do you need help?" she said.

"Help?"

My brain didn't seem to work, and I couldn't think of anything else to say. I really didn't want to look like a fool, but it was too late for that.

"Perhaps you've been in the sun too long," she said. "Come with me."

She put a gentle hand on my shoulder and directed me inside the store. I had been in Aunt Maude's store at least a thousand times, but I hardly recognized the place.

"What's your name?" she said.

"Shirley," I said. "Shirley Ivey."

"It is very nice to meet you, Shirley."

More graceful than anyone I had ever seen, she practically glided across the floor. I was mesmerized by the woman.

She led me to a bookcase where canned goods shelves used to be. Next to it, where the postal counter once was, were two brocade-covered easy chairs.

"I'm Elaine Carter," she said, motioning toward one of the chairs. "Please, come and sit for a while."

It had been an exhausting morning dealing with Grandpa's truck and that Betty person. I couldn't think of a single reason why I shouldn't sit down and rest.

"You said your last name is Ivey?"

Miss Carter eased herself onto the other chair. She kept her eyes on me as though I were some sort of specimen. I was acting so strangely I couldn't blame her, and I found her concern comforting.

"Yes," I finally said. "My grandmother owns the café across the street."

"I met your grandmother," she said. "She is a lovely woman."

"Thank you."

"She mentioned you would be coming this summer."

"She did?"

I scanned the store for other changes, and there were a lot of them. It no longer looked like Aunt Maude's general store, and I liked what I saw.

"What kind of place is this?"

Miss Carter's face lit up. Her wide smile revealed perfectly aligned teeth.

"It is a place where people may come to relax."

She waved her arm toward the opposite side of the room. There were two overstuffed sofas facing each other and a coffee table between them.

"It's really pretty," I said, "and comfortable."

"Thank you," she said. "I have worked tirelessly to achieve that effect."

I still didn't know what the place was. The sofas and coffee table made it feel like somebody's living room.

"While my guests drink their favorite coffee, they may sit and read a book or a newspaper."

What did she say? Did my ears hear correctly? Did she say coffee and newspapers?

If that's what she said, she had my full attention. All my instincts warned me to proceed carefully.

"I don't understand, Miss Carter."

"It's an idea I saw in practice in larger cities," she said. "I don't see why the residents of Willowdale shouldn't enjoy the same amenities."

"You mean like reading a newspaper while drinking a cup of coffee?"

"That's correct," she said, "but I serve several flavors of coffee instead of only one."

"There are different flavors of coffee?"

"Yes," she said, "and I have an extensive collection of books for them to enjoy."

I looked around the room. There were three floor-to-ceiling bookcases, and every shelf was lined with books. I didn't know how anyone could read all of them in a single lifetime.

"Do you serve food, too?"

"Not at the moment," she said, "but I do plan to offer pastries in a week or two."

"What kind of pastries?"

"I believe I'll begin with cinnamon rolls and coffee cake," she said. "The usual breakfast items most people enjoy."

I couldn't believe what I heard, but I knew I wasn't comfortable anymore. Without knowing it, I had stumbled into the enemy's camp.

"My grandma already has newspapers and a place to sit and read them."

"Yes, of course," she said. "However, her café doesn't offer as luxurious a place to read as my coffee shop."

"No, I suppose it doesn't."

I had to admit the changes she made to Aunt Maude's store were gorgeous and inviting. The sofas and chairs scattered around the room were plush, and the floor was highly polished. The whole space felt like a library and a cozy living room all at the same time.

The smell of freshly brewed coffee added to the cozy feeling. I understood how her store would appeal to a lot of people, and that's what worried me.

"My coffee shop is called "Elaine's", and the outdoor sign will arrive in a day or two."

That did it. I heard all I needed to hear about her store and all her plans. I jumped to my feet and practically sprinted to the front door.

"Thank you for letting me rest," I said. "I have a lot of work to do."

I was pretty sure she didn't want to know what I thought about her and her coffee shop. I got the impression her plans were purposely designed to destroy Grandma's business.

I didn't bother to say good-bye. I ran out the door as though my saddle oxfords were on fire. I couldn't get to the café fast enough.

"There's a lot of work to do alright," I said to myself.

I had to warn Grandma. We needed to come up with a plan to keep "Elaine's" from taking business away from Ivey's Café.

Six

When I got to the café, I burst through the front door. I wanted to speak with Grandma in private about Miss Carter's plans.

My timing couldn't have been worse. The café was jammed with customers, and the volume of conversations was deafening. In the midst of the chaos, Grandma was at one of the tables taking an order.

"Shirley," she said. "There you are."

She glanced at me and wrote on her order pad at the same time. It was clear my talk with her would have to wait.

I hurried to the kitchen and tied a clean apron over my blouse and jeans. After I washed my hands at the prep sink, I rinsed out a table rag.

Irene was at the stove pouring one ladleful of batter after another onto the griddle. I didn't want to interrupt her, so I turned around and hurried back to the dining room.

It had been months since I worked with Grandma, but I still remembered the routine. When Irene had an order ready, one of us delivered it to the correct table. Between orders, we both bused tables or poured coffee. The only job Grandma insisted on doing herself was running the cash register.

After I bused my first table, I passed Grandma with my hands full of dirty dishes. She was taking an order, and I whispered to her as I hurried by.

"What's going on?"

She looked up and said, "A bus load headed for Lafayette."

Grandma was in her element. She loved to stop at every table and visit with every customer while she took orders. Before the café closed, she would know life stories and personal secrets about most of them.

It wasn't as though she pried for information because she didn't. People were naturally drawn to Grandma and felt comfortable speaking freely to her.

"Wow, you having a bake sale or something?"

It was Jim near the front door, shouting at me over the din. Before I could say a word, Betty stepped inside and stood next to him.

"When the front table opens up," I said, "grab it before somebody else does."

"Will do," Jim said.

They stood by the door, staring at the three customers at the table. It was embarrassing to watch them, but their tactic worked. In only a few minutes, the strangers finished their breakfasts, paid their bill and left. No more waiting.

Jim plopped down on a chair, and Betty gracefully lowered herself onto the one beside him. I was relieved Jim saw to it she observed the café's long-held custom. No one sat on Grandpa's chair with the green cushion.

The room was hectic, but all the orders were delivered. Only the front table needed cleaning, and I made my way over there with the wet rag.

"Grandma and I can't stop to eat right now," I said. "We don't want you to wait for us."

Betty looked over at Jim and put her hand on his arm. He smiled at her, and she smiled back. I wanted to vomit.

"I guess we better eat now," he said. "Betty has to get over to her aunt's place pretty soon with the picnic basket."

"Oh, yes, the picnic basket," I said. "Did I interrupt your plans this morning?"

I put the rag on the table and began clearing the dirty dishes. It felt odd waiting on people my age.

"Nope," Jim said.

"We drove all over the county this morning collecting wildflowers," Betty said. "The picnic basket keeps them fresh and undamaged."

I couldn't imagine why anybody would want a picnic basket full of wildflowers. I wanted to ask about it, but I didn't want Betty to know I was curious.

"I hope you don't mind," I said. "It looks like pancakes are the bill of fare today."

"Sounds good to me," Jim said. "How about you, Betty?"

Betty looked up at me with her big, blue eyes. She flashed me a wide, perfectly aligned smile and slipped her other hand into one of Jim's.

Forget vomit. I refused to allow her show of affection for Jim to have that much power over me.

"I suppose pancakes are alright," she said, wrinkling her nose, "but tell the cook we're in a hurry."

I stared into her eyes and felt a chill. She had a lot of nerve making demands on Irene over a free breakfast. So, I ignored her and slowly wiped down the table with my free hand.

"You're in a hurry?"

"I am," she said. "I have to get over to Aunt Elaine's before the flowers wilt."

"Aunt Elaine?"

"Yeah," Jim said. "Betty's aunt bought Aunt Maude's store."

Seven

Grandma sat down on the chair next to Grandpa's. She kicked off her laced shoes and rolled down her knee-high nylon stockings. I could tell by her swollen ankles she was on her feet too long.

"It hasn't been this busy since the train depot was in operation," she said.

"Thank the Lord we're still on the bus route," Irene said.

The cook pulled out the chair between Grandma and me and sat down. Her cheeks were red, and she wiped at the perspiration on her forehead with her apron. Split ends jutted out from her braid like a frayed rag rug washed too many times.

"It used to be busier than this?" I said.

"It was when the bus and the train arrived at the same time," Grandma said. "We had a line of customers out the door and down the block."

"A waiting line?" I said. "What did you do?"

"Your grandfather was a very resourceful man," she said. "He walked along the line and sold the waiting customers newspapers or cold drinks."

I laughed at the thought, untied my shoes and kicked them off my feet. With both hands, I grabbed my right foot and laid it across my left knee. I massaged the aching arch with my thumbs.

"What did he do in the winter when it was freezing outside?"

"That was the best of all scenarios for him," Grandma said. "He offered coffee and hot chocolate for sale and invited them to wait in the storeroom."

"Why in the world would he invite anybody into that dirty old room?"

I stopped massaging my foot and furrowed my brow. Grandma nodded her head and laughed a little.

"That was the same reaction I had the first time he mentioned the idea," she said.

Irene looked at me and shook her head. Each time her head moved, her braid wagged back and forth. I was glad to see her face was less red and the perspiration was gone.

"That's the best part of the story," she said. "Tell her, Marie."

Grandma smiled at her cook and sat up a little straighter. One at a time, she put her feet up on the chair across from her. When she was settled, she looked at me.

"You remember how much your grandfather loved people, don't you?"

"Of course," I said. "He thought everyone was his friend."

"Well, every winter he cleared out the storeroom."

"I didn't know that, Grandma."

"I remember," Irene said.

"There is a potbellied stove in the corner," Grandma said. "It's buried under boxes now."

"Okay," I said, "but why did he clear out the room?"

Grandma loosened the top button on her dress and sighed. There was a twinkle in her eyes, and her smile was wider.

"He needed the space when he hosted his friends on Friday nights."

"What was special about Friday night?"

"It was the night they played poker," she said.

"Grandpa played poker?"

"Let her finish," Irene said. "It gets way better."

I put my right foot on the floor and grabbed my left foot. I crossed it over my right knee and massaged the arch.

"During café hours, the room was stocked with games he thought children might like," she said.

"Wow."

"There was even a jigsaw puzzle on the poker table for the adults."

"Everybody loved waitin' in there," Irene said.

"That was pure genius, Grandma."

"That isn't the best part, dear."

She shifted her weight and crossed her feet. There was less swelling in her ankles, but I still worried. She pulled out the hankie tucked behind her belt and fanned her face.

"Are you okay, Grandma?"

"She's okay," Irene said. "Let her finish the story."

Grandma smiled at the cook, but she kept fanning her face. Her cheeks looked too red to me.

"While they waited," she said, "he made certain they knew unopened boxes of the games and puzzles were for sale."

"Grandpa!"

"Your grandpa had a real head for business," Irene said. "Yeah, he did."

"It's true," Grandma said. "We sold a great deal of merchandise in those days."

"Why don't you still have the room open for your customers?"

"That's a real good question," Irene said. "I've been askin' her that myself for two years now."

Grandma looked from me to Irene and back again. A few strands of hair hung from the bun at the nape of her neck. She didn't bother to tuck them back into place.

"The room was Robert's creation," she said. "It wouldn't be the same without him."

"Oh, Grandma, you'd be wonderful at it."

"Besides," she said. "I don't know the first thing about potbellied stoves."

I uncrossed my left foot and lowered it to the floor. Both arches felt better after the massage, but my stomach didn't. It growled, and I instinctively slapped both hands against the waistband of my jeans.

"Sorry," I said. "I guess I'm kind of hungry."

Grandma looked up at the clock. When she looked back at me, she looked horrified.

"Ye gods," she said. "We never did stop to eat, did we?"

"Truth be told, I couldn't stand to cook another pancake," Irene said.

The clock chimed four times, and all three of us looked up at it. Nobody spoke or moved to get up, but we all let out a loud sigh.

After a minute, Grandma stopped fanning her face and tucked the hankie under her belt. She rolled her nylons back up her legs, slipped into her shoes and stood up.

"I couldn't possibly look at another pancake myself," she said.

"What do you want to do, Grandma?"

She looked at Irene, then at me. She smiled, and her eyes sparkled.

"Let's raid the cooler," she said. "Let's cook three of the ground sirloin burgers we're serving for tomorrow's lunch special."

"I volunteer to clean up the kitchen afterward," I said.

"Sounds fair to me," Irene said.

"You have to promise me one thing, Grandma."

"Oh, my," she said. "What might that be?"

I finished tying my shoes, stood up and walked over to her. I put an arm around her shoulders.

"You let Irene do the cooking."

Eight

"What's the matter with me?"

I was exhausted from my first day of work, but I couldn't fall asleep. I tossed and turned, and my eyes wouldn't stay closed.

Instead of lying awake, I crawled out of bed and tiptoed to the built-in seat. I sat down in front of the dormer window and curled my legs up under me.

The tiny bedroom had been my playroom when I was a little girl. I loved how cozy it was, tucked up under the eaves of Grandma's old farmhouse.

The little dormer window was wide open, but it didn't help. Only a light breeze blew in, and the room was stifling.

I knew the air would cool down by morning, and I would need a light blanket. Until then, my thin cotton nightgown was too heavy, and it clung to my skin.

"At least I'm not hungry."

It had been almost dark by the time we finished eating our burgers and cleaning up the kitchen. Irene only walked two blocks to get home, and there were street lights all the way.

Grandma and I weren't that lucky. Since the truck was still being fixed, we were forced to walk over a mile to get home.

Our route was along the same graveled county road we walked along all last summer.

When we got to the farmhouse, Grandma went straight to her bedroom and closed the door. A few minutes later, I heard soft snoring.

"Thank goodness one of us is getting some rest."

With no one to keep me company, I wasn't interested in listening to myself talk. I decided the only solution to my loneliness and the stuffy bedroom was to go downstairs.

"Maybe it'll be cooler on the back porch."

I slipped off the window seat and tiptoed to the dresser across the room. Without turning on a light, I rummaged through the drawers feeling for something to wear.

I finally found a shirt and a pair of shorts. I couldn't see if they matched or not, but I didn't care. I was anxious to get downstairs even though it wouldn't be the same without George.

Last summer, Grandma and I took the little pug home with us every day after the café closed. Because Grandma didn't want hair all over the house, he slept in a cardboard enclosure in the kitchen.

If I got up for snacks during the night, I let him out. He kept me company, but he wouldn't be there for me anymore.

When I went home to South Bend, George went to live with Jim and his father at the mill. The enclosure and all his things went with him. I didn't like that arrangement, but he was Aunt Maude's dog. That's the way she wanted it, and I had no right to complain.

"I'm definitely going to Mr. Spencer's mill in the morning to check on you, big guy."

I felt my way down the stairs and along the hallway to the back of the house. The air was cooler the closer I got to the kitchen. It was a sure sign the back door was still open.

When I got to Grandma's bedroom, I stopped, held my breath and listened. She was still snoring softly, so I tiptoed past her closed door.

In the kitchen, I eased the screen door open just wide enough to squeeze through. I stepped out onto the porch in my bare feet.

I didn't usually go outside without shoes in case I stepped on a bug. On such a warm night, however, the coolness of the concrete felt wonderful.

It was pitch black, and I swung my arms ahead of me, feeling for the nearest chair. Before I took two steps, I heard a scraping sound in the direction of the garage. I stopped and stood very still.

I imagined the night full of wild creatures and waited for the sound to come again. It didn't.

I walked forward again, bumped into a lawn chair and sat down. The coolness of the metal seat felt good against my bare legs.

I regretted not wearing my shoes. It was the perfect evening to sit on the old porch swing Grandpa hung from a tree for me. That was where George and I sat every day after work last summer.

"I'm not going upstairs to get my shoes now," I said to myself. "I'll go out to the swing tomorrow."

I leaned against the back of the seat and rested my arms on the chair's armrests. A breeze blowing off the cornfield behind the house was cool against my skin. I closed my eyes and breathed in the fresh air.

I was almost asleep when I heard the scraping sound again. It was followed by a soft whimper.

My eyes shot open, and I sat straight up. I wasn't relaxed anymore.

"Who's out there?" I whispered, imaging monsters of every shape and size descending upon me.

When no one answered, I jumped to my feet. I opened the screen door, reached for the wall switch and snapped on the overhead porch light.

I expected to see an intruder standing at the bottom of the porch steps. I was prepared to scratch his eyes out, but no one was there.

Still, I heard scraping and another whimper. The sounds definitely came from the direction of the garage. This time, I didn't bother to whisper.

"Who's there?"

Besides the scraping and whimpering near the garage, I heard scuffling sounds in the kitchen. When I turned around, Grandma was at the door. She was dressed in slippers and a floor-length nightgown, and she held a flashlight in one hand.

"What's going on out here?" she said. "I heard you call to someone."

"Sorry I woke you up."

"Nonsense," she said. "I'm glad you did."

She opened the door a crack and handed me the flashlight. I clicked it on. The batteries were old, and the beam was yellow.

"You stay there, Grandma," I said. "I heard noises by the garage."

"Why are you out there on the porch?"

"I came down to cool off."

"I see."

I swung the pitiful beam back and forth along the length of the small, limestone building. I didn't see anything at first.

On the last swing, I saw some movement. Something disturbed the grass along the foundation at the far end of the garage. The beam was just too weak for me to see what was out there.

"Did you see that, Grandma?"

"See what, dear?"

I held the beam very still and waited to see if my eyes were playing tricks on me. Only a moment later, I saw it again.

"There."

Something rustled the untrimmed grass. That proved my eyes were fine, and it wasn't my imagination. I only needed to decide if I really wanted to do anything about it.

Grandma came outside, closed the screen door behind her and stood next to me. After a few seconds, I made my decision and handed her the flashlight.

"Keep the light on the grass, Grandma," I said. "I'll go put on some shoes."

"What should I do if it moves again?"

"Don't do anything," I said. "I'll be right back."

I left her there with the flashlight and ran up to my bedroom. It only took a minute to slip into my old moccasins and run back to the porch.

"The grass keeps moving a little," Grandma said. "It's too dark for me to see what's causing it."

I took the flashlight from her and started down the steps. I hoped I would only find the neighbor's cat, not a rat or a skunk. One thing was for sure, I would never rest until I found out what it was.

Just in case, I mentally inventoried Grandma's pantry. I figured she had just enough tomato juice in there to handle a skunk incident. How lucky for me.

The garage was only fifty feet or so from the porch, but I took my time getting there. I didn't know what to expect, and I wasn't in a big hurry to find out.

"Be very careful out there, young lady," Grandma said. "Don't hurt yourself."

I didn't intend to get hurt, but my heart beat faster and faster. I think I held my breath.

As I got closer to the moving grass, the scraping and whimpering grew louder. My heart raced faster. Before I fainted from lack of oxygen, I took a deep breath.

"What am I getting myself into?" I said to myself.

Three feet from the garage, I stopped. My mouth dropped open.

"What in the world?"

"What is it, Shirley?"

I was both relieved and horrified at what I saw. Right in front of me was Aunt Maude's precious pug, scratching at the foundation. After each scratch, he bumped his head against the concrete and whimpered.

"It's George, Grandma," I said. "It's George."

My heart broke at the sight of him and tears poured down my cheeks. I knelt down and gently placed my hand on his back. He stopped struggling and looked up at me with his clouded eyes.

"Oh, George, what are you doing here?"

His tail wasn't curled up like a little clock spring. It hung down, tucked between his hind legs. His tongue hung from the side of his open mouth, and his breathing came in quick gasps.

"Oh, George."

I dropped the flashlight in the lawn, scooped him into my arms and held him against my chest. His little body trembled.

To reassure him he was safe with me, I did the only thing I knew to do. I leaned down and gave him a gentle kiss on the top of his head.

"Oh, big guy," I said. "What happened to you?"

I didn't waste precious time trying to guess. I stood up and cradled him in my arms all the way back to the house.

Nine

Grandma was waiting on the porch for us with a beach towel. We wrapped George in it and took him inside the house.

While I held him close to me, Grandma hurried to the telephone on the kitchen wall. Even though she was tethered to the receiver by the phone cord, she paced. She didn't stop until Miss Spitz came on the line.

"Harriet," she said to the operator. "You must call Dr. McCray immediately."

Grandma watched George and me as I circled the kitchen trying to calm the little pug. When that didn't work, I sat down on one of the kitchen chairs.

I gently rocked back and forth as if I were sitting in a rocking chair. With my lips close to his ear, I hummed the only lullaby I knew.

"If you can't find him, try Dr. Thompson," Grandma said into the receiver.

"What is it, Grandma?"

"Ye gods," she said. "It seems Dr. McCray isn't coming to Willowdale for another two days."

She had no patience with anyone who wasn't available when she needed something. Being a traveling veterinarian wasn't an acceptable excuse.

"Dr. Thompson isn't a veterinarian," I said.

"He has been helping to care for George since you left," she said. "I'm certain he'll come when he learns Maude's dog needs help."

She continued to pace in front of the phone with the receiver pressed to her ear. When the doctor came on the line, she stopped pacing and practically yelled into the phone.

"Hurry, Doctor," she said. "I'm afraid George is in a bad way."

Grandma hung up the phone without saying good-bye and went into her bedroom. A few seconds later, she was back wearing a robe and carrying a bed sheet. She threw the sheet over the kitchen table and brushed out the wrinkles.

While we waited, I kept rocking George on my lap and humming the same silly song. He seemed to like it. His trembling stopped, and he relaxed his full weight against my chest.

Grandma paced back and forth again. This time between the wall phone and the kitchen sink. Every time she passed by the screen door, she peeked outside.

It seemed like hours, but it was really only minutes before Dr. Thompson arrived. When he stepped onto the porch, Grandma opened the door before he could knock.

Without any hesitation, the doctor swept right by her and straight over to George and me. He had his black leather bag, and I could tell by his frown he was concerned.

"Put him on the table, Shirley," he said. "I'll have a look."

I loosened my grip and gently placed George on the table in front of the doctor. The little pug rolled onto his side and yawned. His trembling was gone, and his breathing wasn't as labored. I was certain those were positive signs.

Grandma and I stood beside the table and watched Dr. Thompson examine George. He listened to his chest with a stethoscope and shined a light into each of his eyes.

When he was finished, I rested my hand on George's side to reassure him. I wanted him to know I was there, and I wasn't going to leave.

"Well, Doctor," Grandma said. "What is your prognosis?"

"This boy has been through quite an ordeal tonight," he said. "Especially, if he walked all the way from Bill Spencer's mill."

"I guess he must have," I said. "Is he going to be okay?"

"It would help if I knew exactly what happened."

"I'll call Bill right now," Grandma said. "Maybe he can shed some light on this mystery."

"Good," he said. "We need answers."

When Grandma went to the phone to call Mr. Spencer, my imagination ran wild. I thought about the dangers George faced getting to Grandma's house, and I got angry.

Jim had a lot to explain, but confronting him over the phone wasn't good enough. I needed to deal with him face to face.

"George is a very lucky dog," the doctor said.

"What do you mean?"

He paused for a moment and looked me in the eye. His brow was still furrowed, and when he spoke there was no humor in his voice.

"George is over eleven years old," he said. "If you hadn't found him, I don't believe he would have lasted the night."

Tears welled up in my eyes at the thought. Dr. Thompson was trying to reassure me, but he wasn't making me feel any better.

Aunt Maude wanted her little pug to stay in Willowdale to be near his human friends. She trusted Jim to make a home for George and take good care of him. What would she think if she knew he let her down?

"What do we do now, Doctor?"

"Keep him quiet for the rest of the night," he said. "A little water would be alright."

"What about tomorrow?"

"By morning, he should be ready for something to eat."

I bent over and gave George a gentle kiss behind his ear. He lifted his head and gave me a sloppy kiss on my nose.

"Why do you think he was trying to get into the garage?"

"It won't be long before he's totally blind from cataracts," he said. "He was probably searching for the house and thought he was at the back steps."

I picked George up from the table and held him close. The thought of him wandering half-blind around the countryside made me sick to my stomach.

"He'll be safe here, Doctor," I said. "You can be sure we'll take good care of him."

"I know you will," he said, putting a hand on my shoulder. "Just remember to take care of yourself, too."

Dr. Thompson tucked the stethoscope and flashlight inside his leather bag and walked to the back door. He stopped just long enough to see that Grandma was still on the phone.

"Say good night to your grandmother for me," he said. "Tell her I want to see George tomorrow morning for a follow-up exam."

"We'll be there," I said. "Thank you so much for coming."

After the doctor left, I laid George on the bed Grandma made for him. As soon as his body touched the blanket, he rolled onto his side and fell asleep.

"Don't worry, big guy," I said. "I won't let anything bad happen to you ever again."

I stretched out on the floor next to him and watched his chest rise and fall. Watching him sleep relaxed me, and my eyelids grew heavy. I didn't remember falling asleep.

Ten

"Listen, Jimmy, you need to get yourself over to Mrs. Ivey's café right now."

His son pulled his baseball cap off his head and slapped it against his pant leg. He ran his hand back and forth across the top of his crew cut.

"I can't," he said.

"What do you mean you can't?"

"When I get done with my paper route, I'm helping Betty pick more flowers for her aunt."

"You mean to tell me you think picking flowers is more important than checking on George?"

"It's a job, Dad," he said. "Miss Carter pays me to do it."

"So, the job is more important?"

His son stopped running his hand across his crew cut. He let out a loud sigh, rolled his eyes and settled his cap back on his head.

"No," he said, "but when you talked to Mrs. Ivey last night, she told you he'd probably be okay."

Bill reached out and grabbed his son by the arm. When he tried to pull away, Bill tightened his grip.

"I don't know what's come over you," he said. "George was your responsibility, remember?"

"I know that, Dad," he said, twisting his arm free. "I can't watch him every second."

Bill turned a packing crate up on its end and sat down. He was tired of reasoning with his son.

"Nobody expected you to watch him every second," he said.

"So, what's the problem?"

"The problem?" Bill said. "You were so busy thinking about your girlfriend, you forgot to close the delivery door."

"How was I supposed to know he'd run away?"

"You know he doesn't like to be alone."

"Yeah, but—"

"He was probably looking for you."

"Well, he found Shirley," he said. "That was good."

Bill rubbed his hands together trying to ease the ache in the swollen, arthritic joints. He didn't know which was worse— the pain in his hands or the pain in his heart over his son's callousness?

"With his bad eyes," Bill said, "it's a miracle he didn't get hit by a car."

His son crossed his arms in front of his chest and looked at the floor. He scuffed the toe of his tennis shoe against a crack in one of the boards.

"It won't happen again," he said. "I promise."

"No, it won't."

He stopped kicking the broken board and looked up. Bill saw the confusion on his face.

"What's that supposed to mean?"

"George is staying with Shirley and Mrs. Ivey from now on."

His son dropped his arms to his sides and moved a step closer. His hands were rolled into fists.

"They can't do that," he said.

"Yes, they can," Bill said. "Aunt Maude wanted both you and Shirley to look after him."

"It was just an accident, Dad."

"Maybe so, but you'll never get Mrs. Ivey or Shirley to see it that way."

Before Bill could say anything more, Shirley barged through the delivery door. She walked by his son without saying a word and stopped in front of him.

Bill thought she looked all cheery in her jeans and bright yellow blouse. However, the expression on her face didn't match the mood of her clothes. He had never seen her look so angry.

"I've come to get George's food and his bowls you borrowed from Grandma," she said.

"Good morning, Shirley," Bill said. "How's our little boy doing today?"

"Dr. Thompson checked him out again this morning," she said. "He thinks he'll be fine after a lot of rest."

His son didn't say anything to Shirley. He relaxed his fists and took a step back.

"See, Dad?" he said. "Mrs. Ivey knew he'd be okay."

Shirley jammed her fists on her hips and spun around to face him. Her voice was ice-cold.

"What do you care, Jim?" she said. "All you think about is that Betty person and her aunt's new store."

"That's not true."

"Isn't it?" she said. "George could have died last night."

"But he didn't."

"You didn't even bother to call back after Grandma talked to your father."

"I didn't think I had to."

Her face turned bright red, and she widened her stance. Bill could see she wasn't finished.

"Aunt Maude put you in charge of her little pug," she said, "and all you can say is 'I didn't think I had to'."

"Well, I didn't," he said. "Dad told me everything your grandma said."

"Did he tell you George isn't coming back here again?"

She turned away from him. Her face was still bright red.

"If you don't mind, Mr. Spencer, I'll take those bowls and the food now."

With a groan, Bill pushed himself up from the crate. He led her to a small area beside the delivery door.

"There're the bowls your grandma gave us," he said, "and that's the blanket George likes to sleep on."

When she finished gathering everything off the floor, he pointed to a bag of dog kibble on a small shelf. She grabbed that, too.

"Anything else?" she said.

"No," Bill said. "That's all there is."

With her arms heaped with George's belongings, she spun on her heel and left the mill without saying good-bye. His son didn't try to stop her or offer any help.

Bill managed to get to the door in time to see her step off the bottom of the delivery ramp. She turned up the road toward Willowdale without a backward glance.

"You're a good girl, Shirley," he said under his breath. "Your grandma's lucky you're here."

Eleven

"Move that box and that box and that box."

Grandma stood in the doorway of the café's storeroom and barked orders at Mr. Martin and me. I seemed to be the only one with enough nerve to question her choices.

"Are you sure you want to move all these boxes to the garage?" I said. "George doesn't need much room."

"Young lady," she said. "We want our little boy to be comfortable, don't we?"

"Of course, but—"

"Get busy," she said. "I want this room cleared by the time we close for the day."

She walked into the dining room, leaving the two of us alone. We had moved boxes since the last breakfast customer left, and I needed a break.

Mr. Martin groaned, pulled a rumpled handkerchief from his pants pocket and mopped his forehead. He looked exhausted.

"I swear yer grandma's tryin' ta kill me."

I wanted to laugh at him, but it hurt too much. My back ached from lifting boxes and from sleeping on the kitchen floor next to George all night.

"I think she's trying to kill both of us," I said.

I didn't mind clearing the room and moving everything to Grandma's garage. If that's what Grandma wanted, that's what she would get.

I just didn't understand why we needed to move every box out of the storeroom. All George needed was a little space for his blanket and his bowls.

Irene was in the kitchen banging spatulas against steel pans and chopping something on the cutting board. My mouth watered at the thought of food.

"Sounds like Irene's working hard, too," I said.

I imagined the day's sirloin burger special on a plate heaped with French fries. My stomach punished me for the thought by growling.

Mr. Martin didn't seem to notice. He continued to wipe at his forehead.

George was on his blanket next to the door to the small bathroom. As usual, he was on his back and asleep.

Mr. Martin looked over at him. He lowered his handkerchief, shook his head and groaned.

"Thought yer grandma didn't allow dogs in here."

I didn't mind if he called me a city girl. I didn't even mind if he blamed me for Grandma's idea to clear the storeroom.

The one thing I did mind was him taking his frustrations out on George. The little pug didn't deserve that, and it wasn't any of his business anyway.

"Grandma says he's coming with us every day from now on," I said.

Mr. Martin responded by grumbling something under his breath. I couldn't make out what it was.

"Besides," I said. "George isn't a dog, he's family."

He stuffed his handkerchief back in his pocket and sat down on the nearest box. His old felt hat was pushed back on his head.

"How're we gonna git all this ta the garage anyways?" he said. "Yer grandpa's truck's broken."

I wondered about that myself. Before I could think of a reasonable answer, there was a knock on the back door.

I didn't expect Mr. Martin to get up, so I stepped around him and opened it. Mr. Spencer stood just outside with his hat in his hands.

"Your grandma called me."

"I sure am glad to see you," I said.

He looked like an angel in khaki pants and work boots coming to our rescue. His truck was backed up to the steps and empty of the usual grain sacks and debris.

"Let's load up these boxes," he said. "We'll get them up to the garage in no time."

"What about George?" I said. "Can he come along?"

"I'd never leave him behind," he said.

Mr. Martin grumbled under his breath again. I still couldn't understand what he said, so I shrugged my shoulders and ignored him.

Thank goodness Mr. Spencer understood how I felt about George. The thought of taking him with us perked up my spirits, and I ignored my sore back. I walked over to his truck and climbed into the bed.

For the next half-hour, the three of us worked like a well-ordered bucket brigade—in slow motion. Mr. Martin brought the boxes to the back door, and Mr. Spencer carried them over to me. I stacked the boxes, two-high, from the front of the truck bed to the back.

When the last box was loaded, I stood in a small space I left empty by the tailgate. I admired how neatly everything was stacked and felt proud of the work the three of us did.

After a couple of minutes, Mr. Martin and Mr. Spencer came outside. They climbed into the cab of the truck, but neither of them had George.

I started to jump out to go get him, but I stopped when the back door opened. Clyde Wilson came outside with a grocery bag in one arm and George in the other.

"Your grandma thinks you might want to take him along."

"Thanks, Clyde."

I reached over and took the little pug from him. He was still half-asleep, and he relaxed in my arms.

"And here," he said, placing the grocery bag beside my feet. "Irene says you need something good to eat."

"What is it?"

"Lunch."

He gave George a quick pat on the head and walked to the back door. Before he went inside, he looked back at me.

"That dog needs a bath," he said.

I nodded in agreement. George definitely needed a bath. I planned to give him one before I went to bed.

I sat down in the empty space with dusty George on my lap. I peeked inside the grocery bag, and my stomach rumbled.

"You all set back there?" Mr. Spencer said.

The boxes blocked my view of the cab's window, so I couldn't see either of the men. I rolled down the top of the grocery bag and smiled in their direction.

"Are we ever," I said and gave George a big hug.

Twelve

Marie wrung her hands and walked the perimeter of the storeroom. The potbellied stove looked alright except for soot on the window in the door. The floor was only scuffed a little, but the window on the back wall was black with stove smoke.

"A little paint and a little soap and water will do wonders for the place," she said to herself.

For the first time since Shirley arrived, she had a goal. She was determined to make their last summer in Willowdale a productive one.

She closed the storeroom door and walked to the phone in the dining room. The sign above it warned her customers it should be used only in case of emergencies.

"I think saving the café from bankruptcy qualifies as an emergency."

Clyde Wilson was the only customer in the café and sat at the counter drinking coffee. Marie knew it could be her only chance to make a call before Shirley returned. She had to trust Clyde wasn't a gossip.

She picked up the receiver and waited for the operator. When Harriet came on the line, she asked her to ring Pastor Lawrence at the First Community Church. He answered on the first ring.

"Well, Marie," he said. "What can I do for you?"

"Do you remember Robert's poker table you borrowed for your last bake sale?"

"How could I forget?" he said. "It was a generous thing for you to do so soon after Robert's passing. I stored it downstairs just as you asked me to do."

"I hope it won't be an inconvenience for you to return it."

There was a pause on the other end of the line. It was her table. She didn't understand why he hesitated.

"Let me get this straight," he said. "You want Robert's poker table back in the café?"

"That's correct."

"I shouldn't pry," he said, "but are you starting up the Friday night poker games again?"

Marie laughed at the thought. She didn't know the first thing about card games.

"Would that be a problem?" she said.

There was another pause before the pastor answered. She could just image him wrestling with the type of counsel he wanted to give her.

"Just a little advice," he said. "Whatever you plan to do, keep your wits about you and don't get in over your head."

"Thank you," she said. "I'll keep that in mind."

The pastor was a sweet and kind young man. She hated to leave him with the impression she was about to become a gambler. She just didn't want to reveal her actual plans until they were complete.

"Robert's truck is still at the garage," she said. "Is there any way you could deliver the table to the café today?"

"Today?"

"If it isn't too much trouble."

There was another pause, and she heard papers rustling. She couldn't imagine what he was doing.

"I have my choir member list right here," he said. "There are four older boys who might be able to help."

"Shall we say around four o'clock?"

"Four o'clock?"

"Perhaps they could come before choir practice."

There was another long pause, and again, Marie waited. She didn't know why he needed time to consider her request.

"I suppose that would work."

"Thank you, Albert," she said. "Have them bring the table through the back door and leave it in the storeroom."

Marie hung up the phone and walked to the back of the café. With the poker table taken care of, her mind turned to other concerns.

She needed paint and brushes for the project. She was certain Bill wouldn't mind driving Shirley to Monticello to buy them. He probably had an errand or two he needed to do anyway.

"I'll have Mr. Martin scrub the floor before the boys arrive," she said to herself. "Shirley and I can wash the stove glass and that filthy window."

"Did you say somethin', Marie?"

Irene peeked around the kitchen door. Her hands were covered in soapsuds, and a dishtowel was draped over her shoulder.

"Just thinking out loud is all."

"You better be careful," she said. "They say you know you're crazy when you start answerin' yourself."

"Thank you for the warning."

Irene laughed at her own joke and went back to the dishes in the sink. As she walked, she left a trail of soapsuds across the kitchen floor.

When Marie was alone again, she continued with her plans. She estimated she would need one or two older boys to help Shirley paint the walls. It would probably take another two boys to paint the ceiling.

"If I promise them a hearty meal when they're finished, perhaps I'll get several volunteers."

She finally had a firm plan in place, and she relaxed a little. She even forgot about her financial worries for a moment until the phone in the dining room rang.

"Oh, dear," she said. "Who can that be?"

She seldom received calls at the café. When she did, it wasn't usually good news. She hurried to the dining room and picked up the receiver.

Clyde Wilson was still at the counter drinking his endless cup of coffee. She had no choice but to answer the call and trust in his discretion.

"Marie," Harriet said. "Mr. Daily at the bank is calling."

"Oh, my."

"Do you want me to tell him your line is busy?"

Marie was grateful for a good friend like Harriet. However, ignoring her problems with the bank wouldn't get them resolved.

"That won't be necessary," she said. "You may put him on the line."

"If you say so."

She and Robert had known Gene for many years. They considered him a friend, but she understood the fine line between friendship and business. His calls were always about business.

"Yes, Gene," she said. "How may I help you?"

Thirteen

After we delivered the boxes to the farmhouse, Mr. Spencer drove us back to the café. No matter how tired we all were, Grandma probably had more errands for us to do before we called it a day. There never seemed to be an end to the chores she found for us to do.

"What do you think, George?"

With the boxes gone, my back was leaned up against the front of the truck bed. George was curled up on my lap, sleeping. In spite of the bumpy ride, I was tired enough to fall asleep, too.

I didn't have a chance to close my eyes. When we turned onto Main Street, the truck came to a sudden stop. The jolt threw my head against the cab, and George's head popped up.

"What in the world's going on, big guy?"

I heard cheering and clapping coming from somewhere ahead of us. I nudged George off my lap and twisted around until I could see through the window.

"What—?"

A large group of people stood in the street in front of Aunt Maude's old general store. They were blocking traffic and watching two men teetering on two wooden ladders. The men were about half-way up the rungs with something huge balanced between them.

"What're they doing, George?"

I picked him up, and we watched through the window. Even though I had a pretty good view, I couldn't make out what the men were holding.

George must have thought we were playing a game. He wagged his curly tail so hard his entire body moved back and forth. He looked at me with his big, round eyes and licked my chin.

"Oh, George."

Mr. Spencer eased his truck right to the edge of the crowd. He did a slow U-turn and parallel parked in front of the café. Grandma stood on the sidewalk, watching the activity across the street.

As soon as the truck stopped, I put George down and stood up. The little pug stood next to me and leaned against my leg.

"Grandma, what's going on?"

"Just look at that," she said, nodding toward the new coffee shop.

Standing in the truck gave me a clear view over the top of the crowd. The men on the ladders were holding a huge wooden sign. The word "Elaine's" was routed in italicized letters along its full length.

Mr. Spencer slipped out of the cab and lifted George over the side of the truck. He gently placed him on the sidewalk next to Grandma.

"Here we are," he said to the little dog.

I didn't need him to help me to get out of the truck. I walked to the back of the bed and climbed over the tailgate. I used the bumper as a step.

"They've been at this for almost an hour," Grandma said. "It seems Miss Carter isn't pleased with the way they are hanging the sign."

"Sounds kinda fussy ta me," Mr. Martin said.

He stepped up onto the sidewalk, took off his hat and wiped the inside band with his handkerchief. He blew his nose on the same hankie and stuffed it back in his pants pocket.

"I don't know about any of you," Mr. Spencer said, "but I need to sit down."

Mr. Spencer and I joined everyone on the sidewalk, and we all sat down on the bench. George was unfazed by all the commotion. He curled up at my feet and fell asleep.

Only a minute or two later, Irene elbowed her way out the screen door. She carried a tray of steaming cups and offered one to each of us.

"Figured we should have a little somethin' while we watch," she said.

Even though I was full from her delicious turkey sandwiches, there was always room for chocolate. I chose the only cup of hot chocolate on the tray.

Mom didn't allow me to drink coffee at my age anyway. She said it would stunt my growth or give me a bad complexion or something. It didn't matter to me which one it was. Grandpa gave me a sip from his cup one time, and I couldn't stand the taste.

"Thank you, Irene," Grandma said. "This is exactly what we need."

After everyone chose a cup, Irene laid the empty tray on the end of the bench. She sat down with us, and we all sipped our drinks and relaxed in the awning's shade.

Across the street, Miss Carter wasn't relaxed. She hustled back and forth between the two men on the ladders.

She shouted orders at one man, and then she shouted orders at the other one. I wasn't sure if she would ever be satisfied with their work.

"Not that way," she said. "Move it to the left."

Some of the people in the crowd laughed and cheered. Others just stood quietly and watched.

Before long, however, they all moved on, and the street was no longer blocked. Only the five of us on the bench and the sleeping George were left as witnesses.

"There, that's it," Miss Carter said. "Nail it down before it moves again."

She walked over to our side of the street and looked back at her store. With her arms folded across her chest, she nodded.

"What do you think?"

"Who're you talking to?" Mr. Spencer said.

She turned and glared at him. Anyone could see she wasn't in the mood to quibble.

"I don't care which one of you," she said. "Do any of you have an opinion?"

That was a loaded question. In my honest opinion, she was hurting Grandma's business. Unfortunately, that wasn't what she was asking.

"Shirley?" she said.

I studied "Elaine's" in the center of the sign and the flowers routed around the edge. The flowers were painted in true-to-life colors and contrasted perfectly with the purple lettering.

"It's very pretty," I said.

"Yeah," Mr. Martin said. "Real pretty."

"That's why you had my son searching for wildflowers?" Mr. Spencer said.

"Jim has been invaluable," she said. "I wouldn't have known what flowers to include without his help."

Mr. Spencer shook his head and took a long drink of coffee. None of us spoke again until Irene went inside and brought out a fresh pot of coffee. She refilled every cup except mine, set the pot on the tray and sat down.

"Is the thing big enough?" Mr. Spencer finally said.

I choked back a laugh. My mouth was so full, hot chocolate nearly squirted out my nose.

The sign was definitely big enough. It filled the whole space across the front of the building. "Elaine's" was written large enough to rival the size of the lettering on the water tower.

"There's no need to be rude, Mr. Spencer," Miss Carter said.

"No indeed, there isn't," Grandma said.

I waited for her to offer a comment about the sign, but she didn't. She stood up and placed her cup on the tray.

"Shirley and I must get back to work now."

"We do?"

"Yes, we do, young lady," she said. "We have already spent more than enough time out here."

I wanted to stay and watch some more, but I knew better than to argue with Grandma. I picked up the tray and the rest of the cups without saying another word.

Miss Carter didn't say another word either. She turned around and walked across the street to her coffee shop.

"Thank you for staying late again today, Irene," Grandma said.

"It wasn't any trouble," she said, "but I'll be gettin' on home now."

We all watched her start up the street toward her house. When she was about half-way up the block, Grandma turned toward Mr. Martin and Mr. Spencer.

"Thank you for all of your help today, too," she said.

"No need ta thank me," Mr. Martin said. "That's why ya pay me."

"I was glad to help," Mr. Spencer said. "Anytime."

Grandma brushed at the wrinkles in her apron. When she was done, she looked over at Mr. Martin.

"There is one more thing I need you to do before you go home."

"Can't it wait 'til mornin'?"

"No, it can't," she said. "I'm expecting a delivery in half an hour."

"Yes, ma'am."

"I need the storeroom floor swept and scrubbed before it arrives."

"Yes, ma'am."

Mr. Martin groaned and rubbed at his lower back with his hands. I didn't know much about scrubbing floors, but it sounded like a lot of work. I couldn't stand to see a man his age suffer.

"I'll help him, Grandma."

She smiled at me, but her eyes didn't sparkle. There was definitely something troubling Grandma.

"I'll be on my way," Mr. Spencer said. "Jimmy should be done with his chores by now if Betty hasn't been bothering him."

I wondered where she was, but I didn't want to ask. If she failed to help her aunt hang the new sign, it wasn't any of my business.

Mr. Spencer climbed into the cab of his truck and started the engine. Before he could drive away, Grandma stepped up to the open passenger window.

"There is one thing, Bill," she said.

"What is it?"

"Would you drive Shirley to Monticello tomorrow to buy some paint and brushes?" she said. "You may as well pick up the café's milk while you're there."

"As soon as Jimmy gets home from his paper route, I'd be glad to," he said. "I need to pick up some things for the mill anyway."

"Paint and brushes, Grandma?"

She didn't explain. Instead, the three of us watched Mr. Spencer drive up Main Street and pull onto the road leading to the mill. When he went out of sight, Grandma turned to Mr. Martin and me.

"Let's get to work."

Grandma led us all into the café and to the back of the dining room. She took the tray from me and disappeared into the kitchen.

George wandered over to his bed by the bathroom. He roughed up the blanket into a pile and plopped down on top of the mess. Within seconds, he was asleep.

"You sure are one lucky dog, George," I said under my breath.

Mr. Martin and I stopped at the door of the storeroom. I was tired, and the empty room looked bigger to me than it did before. I was almost sorry I offered to help.

"I'll git the mop an' bucket," he said. "You git the broom an' the funnies outa one of the old papers."

I stared at him for a second, digesting what he said. Was he serious, or was he playing games with me?

"I understand the broom part," I said, "but why the funnies?"

"City girls," he said. "Ya gotta scoop up the dirt with somethin'."

"Yes, but—"

"Ya oughta have somethin' fun ta read while yer doin' it."

Fourteen

Mr. Martin and I finished sweeping and scrubbing just in time. Before the floor was completely dry, four boys from the church delivered Grandpa's poker table.

Grandma circled the storeroom and supervised the move. She had them place the table in several locations before she was satisfied.

While the three of us admired the table, the boys edged toward the door. They almost made it to freedom before Grandma saw them.

"Wait, boys," she said. "I have something for you."

"We don't need anything, Mrs. Ivey," one of them said.

Grandma dismissed that notion with a wave of her hand. She went to the kitchen and brought back a plate piled high with Irene's meat loaf sandwiches.

Without a moment's hesitation, each boy grabbed one from the plate. They didn't wait to start eating.

"It's my thank you for all your help."

"Yes, ma'am," the youngest one said.

While they ate, Grandma eased them toward the back door and said, "Pastor Lawrence is waiting for you at the church."

"Yes, ma'am," they said in unison.

Without a backward glance, they rushed out the door and down the back steps. It looked as though they were escaping before Grandma thought of something else for them to do.

"It's time for you to leave, too, Mr. Martin," she said.

There was no argument from him. He took one of the remaining sandwiches and hurried out the back door.

Grandma carried the plate and the last two sandwiches into the dining room. When we got to the front table, she kept one of the sandwiches and handed the other one to me.

We sat down and kicked off our shoes. I started to eat my sandwich, but Grandma left hers on the plate.

"Aren't you hungry, Grandma?"

"It was a long day," she said. "I'm too exhausted to eat."

I didn't want to be rude, so I laid my half-eaten sandwich on the plate with hers. I closed my eyes and tried not to think about how delicious the meat loaf was.

The only sounds in the café were the ticking of the clock and George's gentle snoring. I leaned against the chair's backrest and relaxed.

"By the way, dear," Grandma said. "There is something extremely important I would like to discuss with you."

My eyes popped open. She had been quieter and more serious than usual. I hoped she was ready to tell me what was bothering her.

"What is it Grandma?"

"I received a very troubling call today."

"Okay."

She loosened the top button on her dress and put her feet on the chair across from her. Her face was drawn into a frown.

"It was Gene Daily at the bank."

"Okay."

She dropped her feet to the floor and pushed herself up from the chair. When she walked to the front window without her shoes, she looked small and vulnerable.

"It seems I'm in quite a financial predicament," she said. "More than I realized."

"What?"

"According to Gene, I owe the bank a great deal of money."

I knew something was worrying Grandma, but I never expected that. It felt like something kicked me in the stomach and sucked all the oxygen out of the room.

"How can that be?" I said.

"Great Grandma and Grandpa Ivey were excellent business people," she said. "They were also generous to a fault."

I tried to comprehend what she said, but it didn't make any sense. How could generosity be a fault?

"What do you mean, Grandma?"

"Sometimes their friends found themselves struggling financially," she said. "Your great grandparents took out loans against the house and the café to lend them money."

"Wow."

She turned away from the window and walked back to the table. Her back was stooped, and she looked as though she aged several years in the last few minutes.

"I still don't understand."

Grandma sat back down. She put her feet up again and leaned against the chair back.

"Over the years, their friends paid them back a little each month plus interest," she said. "All their payments went straight to the bank to pay off the loans."

"If they were charged interest, it was a good deal for Great Grandma and Grandpa."

"Yes, dear, it was a good deal," she said. "Until now."

Seeing Grandma so worried scared me. It was a family matter, but I wasn't even seventeen. She deserved someone older and wiser.

Unfortunately, I was all she had. I needed to be strong for her and think beyond my years.

"The loans aren't getting paid?"

Grandma pulled out the handkerchief from the belt at her waist and mopped her forehead. Her face was pale and her hands shook.

"No, they aren't," she said. "If I don't make them current soon, I'll be forced to sell everything."

My mouth dropped open. Sell the house and the café?

"You have lots of customers," I said. "You must make enough money."

"Some months are better than others," she said. "There just isn't enough money to support both the house and the café."

"And pay off the loans," I said.

"That's right," she said. "And pay off the loans."

I leaned back in my chair. From the looks of the farm-house, I thought my grandparents were rich. I was wrong.

"What does this mean?" I said.

"It means this could be the last summer for Ivey's Café and my last summer in Willowdale."

I couldn't wrap my mind around that possibility. My head hurt just thinking about it.

I wanted to go pick up George and give him a big hug. That always made me feel better, but it would have to wait.

"All their friends are probably gone by now," I said. "Don't their families have to pay back what they owed?"

"All the agreements were made with a handshake."

"Okay."

"Without written contracts to bind them, I assume they aren't obligated."

"Grandpa taught me a man's word is his bond."

"He and your great grandparents truly believed that."

I didn't know which people were involved, but they certainly didn't subscribe to that principle. I wondered if I ever waited on any of them at the café.

"If you sell the house, where will you go?"

"I've been thinking about that," she said. "Maude and I once discussed sharing a home someday."

"You'd move to Illinois?"

"When the loans are paid, I should have just enough funds to move there and pay my share of the living expenses."

Grandma put her hand on mine. Her touch felt cool and not at all reassuring.

"Don't worry, dear," she said.

"I just wish you didn't have to move so far away, Grandma."

She took her hand away and dabbed at her forehead with her handkerchief again. A tiny bit of coloring returned to her cheeks.

"That's why I have decided to reopen the storeroom for the summer," she said. "I want to leave the people of Willowdale with pleasant memories of Robert and me."

"Oh, Grandma, they already have happy memories of you."

She sat up straighter and grinned at me. There was a twinkle in her eyes.

"Perhaps," she said, "but I also want to give Elaine Carter a run for her money before I leave."

"Good for you, Grandma."

Her change in attitude made me feel better. If Grandma could put a positive spin on a bad situation, so could I.

"Can I count on your help, dear?"

I jumped up from my chair and looked outside. The sign on the coffee shop seemed to glare at me, and I laughed out loud.

I couldn't wait for the challenge. Grandma and I would show Miss Carter and her niece how strong and resilient Ivey women were.

"Where do we start?" I said.

Fifteen

Grandma saved the shirt and shorts I wore last summer to paint the water tower. It was a good thing. They were smeared with red paint, and a little taupe on them was barely noticeable.

"It's exactly the right color," I said to myself.

Grandma walked up behind me and put her arm around my waist. We stood in the doorway of the storeroom and surveyed the newly painted walls.

"When the boys finish painting the ceiling," I said, "this will be the prettiest room in the county."

"I think the real beauty is the clean window, don't you?"

I laughed and put my arm across her shoulders. Grandma scrubbed years of dirt and wood smoke from the window. She didn't stop until the glass sparkled.

"You're right, of course," I said.

We stood there for a minute or two and admired all the improvements. Even with the new paint and the clean window, Mr. Martin made the biggest improvement of all. The polish he applied to the old floor boards made the room practically glow.

"Don't you think the floor's dry enough to move George's things in?" I said.

"I believe you're right," Grandma said. "Where shall we put his bed?"

"If we put it by the stove, he'll be able to see into the dining room."

"Where he wouldn't be under foot or bother any of my customers."

"He will still feel like part of the action," I said.

"We will be able to easily check on him throughout the day."

"If we put his bowls next to his bed, he'll get fed on time."

Grandma and I looked at each other. Without another word, it was agreed George would sleep away his days next to the stove.

I picked up the little pug, and Grandma carried his blanket to its new location. When she was satisfied it was folded and placed properly, I laid George on top of it.

"There, big guy," I said. "This is your new room."

He opened his eyes, looked at me for a moment and rolled onto his back. I rubbed his chest while Grandma retrieved his bowls from the hallway and set them beside his blanket.

"It's perfect, dear," she said. "This is exactly where George belongs."

When I stood up, I heard a knock on the door frame. Grandma and I turned around.

Jim stood just outside the room. He held a rectangular-shaped piece of wood with some kind of rope hanging from it.

"Dad told me about all the work you're doing back here," he said.

His blue eyes and wide smile caught me off guard for a second. When I remembered how mad I was at him, I refused to say anything.

"Is there something we can do for you?" Grandma said.

He held up the sign, and I couldn't help but laugh. Grandma smiled and walked over to him.

"Dad made this for you," he said. "He thought you'd like it for your new room."

He stepped forward a few inches and handed her the piece of wood. She held it at arm's length and studied the routed lettering.

"Thank your father for me and tell him the sign is perfect," she said. "I owe him a breakfast whenever he has the time."

"I'll tell him," he said. "Earl says your truck should be ready by tomorrow."

"That is extremely good news," Grandma said. "Thank you."

Jim didn't come into the room or say anything about all our hard work. He turned around and left immediately by way of the back door.

I didn't expect him to say anything to me, but why didn't he speak to George? Maybe he finally understood how disappointed Grandma and I were in him.

I didn't have time to wonder about any of that. Grandma was on the move, and I followed her into the hallway.

Next to the storeroom door, she found an old nail protruding from the plastered wall. She hung the sign by the rope and adjusted it until it was perfectly level.

"Well, dear," she said. "What do you think?"

I stood next to her and studied the sign. The message was the perfect touch, and the sign hung in exactly the right location.

"I love it."

Sixteen

It was a busy Saturday morning. The café was crowded with regular customers and half of the passengers from the morning bus. The other half were across the street at Miss Carter's coffee shop.

Our fear she would siphon off a large number of customers came true. Half or more of every bus load found their way over there. Her business was booming.

"Grandma," I said to myself. "If you want to compete with the coffee shop, you need to get that storeroom open."

I didn't know why she was waiting. The room was painted, the floor was polished and there was a puzzle on the poker table. The easy chairs on either side of the stove made the room as welcoming as someone's home.

"That does it," I said out loud. "It's time someone made an official announcement."

Without discussing it with Grandma, I decided to be that someone. It wouldn't be easy for me.

I hated public speaking. It didn't matter how large or how small the audience thanks to Bradley Jones. Ever since he laughed when I read my poem in sixth grade, I avoided it.

Just the thought of standing in front of the customers made me queasy. I tried to calm myself by taking several deep breaths. I even tried to swallow, but I couldn't. My mouth was as dry as a desert.

"Come on, Shirley," I said. "You can do this."

I willed my feet to carry me to the front of the dining room. I doubted anybody noticed me, but in my mind, I imagined every eye was on me.

"Keep moving," I said under my breath. "You're almost there."

Before I reached the front of the room, Grandma stepped from behind the lunch counter. She was dressed in her navy-blue dress with the lace collar. The one she only wore on special occasions.

Her smile was radiant, and I stopped dead in my tracks. What was she up to?

"Ladies and gentlemen," she said. "Welcome to Ivey's Café."

She stretched her arms out wide and gazed around the dining room. Everyone stopped eating, and the room went silent.

They looked at her, and then at me. It wasn't my imagination all eyes were on both of us. I felt my face turn red.

"My granddaughter and I wish to welcome you to your home away from home."

I forced myself to smile. What in the world was she doing?

"Hey, Mrs. Ivey," Mr. Wilson said around a mouthful of food. "What's goin' on?"

"Yeah," the man next to him said. "What're ya doin'?"

Grandma ignored the two men and continued her speech. She seemed comfortable in front of a room full of people.

"When you have finished your breakfast," she said, "my granddaughter will be happy to show you our game room."

"I will?"

I hated the idea, but Grandma gave me no choice. She put me in charge of showing off her new room, and I wanted to make her proud.

I took a deep breath and pointed to the back of the café. My hands shook, and I couldn't make them stop.

"Come this way," I said. "I'll be—happy to show you."

As I headed toward the back of the café, half a dozen people stood up. They all followed me to the old storeroom.

"This is our game room," I said to the handful of strangers. "Be sure to look at the sign beside the door as you walk in."

I pointed out Mr. Spencer's sign and laughed. One of the women gasped. I knew some people had no sense of humor, but she was being ridiculous.

"Now, Claudia," the man beside her said. "They wouldn't bring us back here if it wasn't safe."

While they all filed into the room, I studied the sign. Didn't they get the joke?

I led them around the entire room. I pointed out the puzzle on the poker table and the boxes of games in the bookcase. Finally, I introduced them to George and offered them a seat in an easy chair.

"Imagine sitting here on a cold day," I said. "The stove will keep you warm while you wait for a table and a home-cooked meal."

"That sounds good, I guess," one of the men said, "but what's up with that poker table?"

"The poker table?"

"The felt on it looks a little worn," he said.

"My grandfather used to play a little poker with his friends."

The man rubbed his chin and nodded his head. After a few seconds, he looked at me.

"What're you going to do with this room when the café's closed for the day?"

"What do you mean?"

"Think about it," he said. "This would be a perfect room to rent out for private parties or club meetings."

I looked around the room with a new set of eyes. He was right. Grandma and I weren't seeing the room's full potential.

"I'll think about it," I said. "Thank you."

He took hold of the gasping woman's arm and steered her toward the door. She looked over her shoulder at me and frowned.

"You might consider removing the dog and getting rid of that sign," she said.

My mouth dropped open, and my hands stopped shaking. She really didn't get it, but I was about to make her understand.

"George is part of our family," I said. "This is his home away from home, too."

The man stopped at the doorway and removed his hand from the woman's elbow. He looked me straight in the eye.

"Don't change a thing," he said.

I had news for him and the gasping woman. I had no intention of changing anything. George wasn't going anywhere, and neither was the "Beware, Guard Pug on Duty" sign.

Seventeen

Elaine and Betty stood at the back of the coffee shop and scanned the room. The bus was about to leave for Monticello, but only a handful of customers waited in her store.

"I'm perplexed," Elaine said. "We should have more guests than this on bus day."

"Maybe it's because Mrs. Ivey opened a game room, Aunt Elaine."

"How do you know this?"

"Jim told me."

Elaine nodded her head. Having that boy work for her and date her niece was working out very well.

"Where in the world would she have the space for that?"

"He says she cleaned out an old storeroom and put it in there."

"Just how well is this game room being received?"

"I guess everybody loves it."

Elaine nodded again and thought about the sweet Mrs. Ivey. When they first met, she felt sorry for the old woman.

She was widowed and ran the café alone. Elaine thought she appeared too inexperienced and too frail to be any competition for the coffee shop.

"It seems I underestimated that woman."

"What do you mean?"

Elaine looked at her niece. Betty liked Mrs. Ivey, and who could blame her? A girl her age would find comfort in the attention of a grandmother figure.

"The lure of a game room most certainly explains why we have fewer guests," she said.

"I suppose so."

"Now, what are we going to do about it?"

Betty turned toward her, and Elaine could read the confusion in her eyes. She almost felt sorry for the girl.

"What can we do about where somebody drinks coffee?" Betty said.

Elaine felt it her duty to teach her niece to be strong and counteract threats to her business. Unfortunately, there wasn't time right then to explain the ruthlessness of the business world.

"We'll discuss it later," she said. "For now, we must make certain our guests' drinks are kept full."

"Yes, Aunt Elaine."

"If they require assistance in retrieving a book or a newspaper, we must never hesitate to help."

"No, Aunt Elaine."

She and her niece scanned the room one more time. There were only two groups of customers.

Three women lounged on the sofas at the front of the store. They discussed the latest fashions and sipped from delicate tea cups.

At the back of the store, two men sat on the brocade chairs. They discussed an article in the newspaper and drank coffee from heavy mugs.

"It appears everyone is content for the moment," Elaine said. "This would be an ideal time for you to brew another pot of coffee."

"Yes, Aunt Elaine."

She watched Betty hurry toward the kitchen, but she wasn't thinking about her niece. She was plotting her next move to recapture the public's interest in her store.

"Game room, Mrs. Ivey?" she said. "We'll just see about that."

Eighteen

"Guard pug?"

Mr. Martin wouldn't stop laughing. He retrieved the wrinkled handkerchief from his pants pocket and wiped at the tears in his eyes.

"You've seen the sign before, Mr. Martin," I said. "It isn't that funny."

Grandma reached over and put her hand on my shoulder. She smiled, and her eyes sparkled.

"Actually, it is," she said. "Bill Spencer was a genius to think of it."

She dropped her hand and walked over to the potbellied stove. As usual, George was asleep and didn't notice when she got close to his bed.

"I asked both of you to stay after closing time to ask your opinion about something."

She had my full attention. Grandma always had the answers to everything. Asking for an opinion about anything from anybody was completely out of character for her.

"What's wrong, Grandma?"

She sat down on the easy chair closest to George and reached down to scratch behind his ears. The little pug yawned and rolled onto his back.

"You little minx," she said. "You are always ready for a tummy rub, aren't you?"

Mr. Martin pulled his felt hat off his head and kneaded its brim. His face was pale, and there were dark circles under his eyes.

"I don't mean ta hurry ya, Mrs. Ivey," he said, "but Jimmy's comin' ta pick me up."

Mr. Martin was a cranky old man at times. He didn't like me very much, but I felt sorry for him since his eyesight went bad.

Not only couldn't he drive for Grandma any more, he was at everybody's mercy. He had to depend on me or Jim or Mr. Spencer to drive him everywhere. Even Pastor Lawrence pitched in to help once in a while.

"I'll come right to the point, Mr. Martin," she said.

Grandma leaned back in the easy chair and sighed. She pulled the handkerchief out from under her belt and dabbed at her top lip.

"A customer told me Elaine Carter expanded her coffee shop into Maude's old apartment."

"Yep," Mr. Martin said. "She turned Aunt Maude's livin' room inta some fancy gift shop."

"Ye gods and little fishes," Grandma said. "Whatever does she sell in her gift shop?"

"Stuff bus people like ta buy."

"Like what?" I said.

"Like fancy tastin' coffee ya gotta grind fer yerself."

"She must sell something other than coffee," Grandma said.

"One time, I saw a lady carryin' smashed flowers in a picture frame."

"I think you mean pressed flowers," Grandma said.

"Pressed flowers," I said. "So that's why Jim and Betty have been picking all those wildflowers."

"Don't matter what ya call 'em," he said. "Folks are buyin' 'em."

"That's too bad," I said.

Grandma shook her head. The sparkle was gone from her eyes.

"There's no denying Elaine knows a great deal about business," she said. "You have to admire her for that."

Admire Miss Carter? Didn't Grandma realize just how amazing she was herself?

"You're just as good at business as she is."

"I try my best," she said. "I'm just afraid this game room isn't as profitable as I hoped it would be."

"It isn't?"

I sat down on the floor next to George, and Mr. Martin plopped down on the other chair. Neither of us said a word and waited for Grandma to speak.

After several minutes, Grandma broke the silence. She sounded tired and defeated.

"Everyone seems to enjoy this room, but no one has purchased a single game or puzzle."

Mr. Martin scooted forward in the chair. He rested his hat on his knee and stared at Grandma.

"What is it ya wanted ta ask us, Mrs. Ivey?"

"I have run out of ideas," she said. "I need your opinion on what to do next to prop up the café's profits."

I had never heard Grandma speak about her problems to anyone outside of the family. It was completely against tradition, and I didn't like it one bit.

"I gotta think on it some," Mr. Martin said.

I already had an idea. It wasn't quite ready to be put into words, but I didn't have a choice. I didn't think Mr. Martin was the appropriate person to rely on to save the café.

"Grandma," I said. "There's something I've been thinking about."

"What is it, dear?"

Mr. Martin groaned, and I was sure he would think my idea was stupid. Maybe Grandma would take me seriously.

"You know the empty lot next door?" I said.

"Yes, dear."

"You never use it for anything."

"No," she said. "Years ago, Frank Riley needed money, and your great grandparents purchased the lot from him."

"Did they ever have plans for it?"

"They only acquired it to help a friend."

"You have to admit it's in pretty rough shape."

Grandma looked me in the eye. I couldn't tell what she was thinking, so I took a deep breath and forged ahead.

"I think we should clean up the lot and knock a hole in the café wall for a door," I said. "After that, we should build a patio and put tables and chairs out there."

I waited for one of them to laugh at my idea. Mr. Martin didn't show any reaction, but Grandma nodded her head slightly.

"Where did you ever get such an idea?" she said.

"Lots of people sit out on their porches in the summer and eat their lunch," I said. "At least they do back home in South Bend."

"It is an intriguing idea," she said, "but how would you suggest we deal with the sun and the rain?"

"Sun an' rain?" Mr. Martin said. "I'm thinkin' flies an' mosquitoes."

I needed to stall for time to think of a way to counter their concerns. I rolled onto my knees and shifted my weight from my right hip to my left. I was beginning to think I shouldn't have said anything.

"Maybe I can figure out a way to solve some of those problems."

Mr. Martin groaned again and slid his hat on his head. He stood up, stuffed his handkerchief back in his pocket and turned toward Grandma.

"I'll keep thinkin' on it," he said, "but I gotta go now."

"I would appreciate any suggestions you have, Mr. Martin," Grandma said. "I believe Shirley's idea has merit."

"Thank you, Grandma."

"However, it does need a bit more work."

That was a positive sign. Grandma took me seriously.

"What if I work on it some more and work out some of the kinks?" I said.

She smiled a little at that. She tucked her handkerchief under her belt and pushed herself up from the chair.

"I am interested in all good ideas," she said.

"Thank you, Grandma."

"Work on your plan a little more," she said. "If you demonstrate how eating outside can lure customers, I will give your idea serious consideration."

Nineteen

I was nervous, and my hands shook. Grandma approved my revised patio plan, and it was about to become real.

Pastor Lawrence rounded up six boys from the church choir to help us with the lot. Because the plan was my idea, Grandma put me in charge of supervising them.

"What do I know about giving orders?" I said.

Grandma looked up from her clipboard and pushed her straw hat up a little higher. Her face glowed with excitement.

"You are going to do just fine," she said.

"I hope so."

We stood in the center of the empty lot wearing wide-brimmed straw hats and leather work gloves. Grandma wore one of her cotton work dresses and a pair of scuffed work shoes. I wore jeans and Grandpa's old dress shirt with the sleeves rolled up.

Even though it was only mid-morning, it was hot. The temperature on the mercury thermometer on the front of the café read 79 degrees in the shade.

"It's getting late," Grandma said. "Don't you think these boys have waited in the sun long enough?"

She was right. It was time to get to work. I took a deep breath and looked into the faces of the boys lined up in front of me.

"We need to pick up all the pop bottles and papers first," I said. "Put everything in the gunnysacks."

I pointed to a stack of the burlap bags Mr. Spencer gave me. They were on the ground next to Grandpa's truck.

"After that's done, who wants to use the sickles and cut down the weeds?"

Two of the older boys raised their hands. They looked muscular enough to play on the high school football team.

"We'll do that."

"Good," I said. "The rest of us will rake up what you cut and throw it in my grandpa's truck."

Grandma checked off something on her list on the clipboard. She looked up at me and smiled.

"I need somebody else to mow what's left with Mr. Martin's push mower," I said.

"I can do that."

One of the younger boys stepped forward. He wasn't much taller than some of the weeds and thinner than I was. I couldn't imagine how he would have the strength to do the job.

"Thank you," I said.

"If you need a break, Lenny, just let me know," one of the other boys said.

"I won't need a break."

Getting them organized was going better than I had hoped. That was probably because of Grandma. She promised them an all-you-can-eat dinner if they minded me and worked hard.

I relaxed a little, and my hands stopped shaking. I couldn't have been more proud of myself than I was at that moment.

"Are there any questions?" I said.

Lenny and another boy scuffed their feet in the dirt and punched each other in the arms. It was obvious they were impatient to get started.

"Alright," I said. "If there aren't any questions, let's get busy."

Grandma watched the boys work while I high-stepped across the lot to the front of the café. Several borrowed rakes were leaned up against the front wall. I grabbed one for Grandma and another one for me.

Before going back to help the boys, I paused to sneak a peek across the street. Two women walked out of the coffee shop with paper bags in their arms.

"Oh, Grandma," I said to myself. "I hope my idea turns out to be as good as I convinced you it was."

There were two figures standing at the front window of the store. I couldn't see them clearly with the sun glaring off the glass. My guess was they were Betty and her aunt.

I couldn't imagine what they thought about the work going on behind me. However, there was one thing I knew for sure. There wasn't an empty lot next door to them.

"Just try and match that, Miss Carter."

When I turned to go back to work, I literally ran into Jim. He was standing on the edge of the sidewalk.

"What are you doing here?" I said, backing up a step. "Spying for Miss Carter and your girlfriend?"

I didn't want to hear anything he had to say, and I tried to brush by him. Before I could, he stepped in front of me and blocked my path.

"Just what do you think you're doing?" I said.

"I want to talk to you" he said. "But you won't give me a chance."

"Why should I?"

He took a step back and jammed his hands into his pockets. The move jarred loose bits of chaff and dust from his clothes.

"I just came from the mill."

"I can see that."

"Dad had me work extra hours today."

"Good," I said, "but you still haven't said what you're doing here."

"I know you're mad at me," he said. "I just thought you and your grandma could use some help."

I moved both rakes to one hand, rested my other hand on my hip and glared at him. I couldn't believe he thought we wanted his help.

"Help us?"

"Yeah, help you clean up this lot."

"Like the way you helped lose George?" I said. "Or like the way you helped tell Betty about Grandma's game room?"

"I'm really sorry about George," he said, "but telling Miss Carter about the game room was just good business. She needs to keep up with the competition, you know."

I couldn't believe my ears. Maybe I didn't know Jim as well as I thought I did.

"Grandma and I are just the competition to you?"

He took his hands out of his pockets and tore his cap off of his head. He swiped his hand across the top of his crew cut, and more dust flew.

"That's not what I meant, and you know it."

I dropped my hand to my side. Did he think I would easily forgive and forget how he neglected George and betrayed Grandma?

"If you're not here to spy for Miss Carter," I said, "why are you here?"

Jim slapped his cap against his pant leg and put it back on his head. He adjusted the bill so the sun wasn't in his eyes.

"I just wanted to help, that's all."

"As I figure it," I said, "if you're not here to spy, you're probably here to sabotage us."

"Sabotage?"

"Maybe Miss Carter wants you to dull the mower blades or loosen the rake tines or—something."

"What?"

I knew I was being ridiculous, but I couldn't stop myself. I wanted him to know how hurt I was.

"What I'm trying to say, Jim, is I don't know how I can trust you."

He threw his hands in the air and stepped backwards a few feet. The expression on his face told me all I needed to know. My unreasonable teenage temper had hurt his feelings, and I wasn't sorry about it.

"All I wanted to do was be friends again," he said.

"I don't know if that's possible as long as you're working for Miss Carter."

I glanced across the street. The two figures were still standing at the window.

I wasn't going to let them intimidate me. I smiled as big as I could and waved at them. They didn't wave back.

"Your friends over there don't seem very friendly today," I said.

I walked away and retraced my steps across the lot back to where Grandma was waiting. I handed one of the rakes to her and stopped to watch the boys work.

"Is everything alright, dear?"

"Everything's fine," I said. "I just needed to settle something with Jim."

The boys had already picked up debris and cut a small section of the lot. They were started on the next section while talking and joking with one another.

"They sure are hard workers, Grandma."

"They're farm boys," she said. "They're used to hard work."

"I suppose so."

Talking to Jim left a bitter taste in my mouth. I decided a little manual labor was just what I needed to get rid of it.

With my rake firmly in hand, I eased my way in among the boys. As soon as I did, they stopped working and stared at me.

I wanted to fit in, not get in the way. I ignored their stares and started raking. For several seconds the only sound was my rake scraping against the rocky soil.

"You're doing a great job," I said to them, "but we could sure use some music while we work."

That eased the tension, and they started raking again. The two older boys began a lively version of "Rock-a My Soul in the Bosom of Abraham". We all joined in and raked in time to the upbeat rhythm.

Twenty

Jim eased his father's truck up the alley behind Ivey's Café and parked parallel to the back door. The truck was slightly hidden by the back steps. He didn't think anyone working on the empty lot could see it.

"So far, so good, Mr. Martin," he said.

The old man sat next to him, kneading the brim of his felt hat. He looked nervous, and Jim couldn't blame him. If they got caught, it could mean the end of his long friendship with Mrs. Ivey.

"Don't ya take long," he said. "Ya never know how long Mrs. Ivey'll be rakin' grass."

"I'll hurry," Jim said. "I promise."

"If she caught me, I'd be in a lota trouble."

"I know."

"If I was in a lota trouble, I'd be out a job."

"I understand, Mr. Martin."

"An' if I'm out a job, I can't keep livin' in my house."

"I won't take long."

"If I can't live in my house, I gotta live with my brother."

"I didn't know you had a brother."

"Ya never met him," he said. "Me an' him don't git along."

"Sorry."

He looked miserable, but it couldn't be helped. He agreed to be the lookout in exchange for a ride home, and Jim was holding him to it.

"You just stay right here," Jim said. "I'll take you home as soon as I'm done."

"I'm not goin' anywhere."

Jim put on his baseball cap and grabbed the wad of waxed paper on the seat. He didn't think his dad would notice a little leftover roast was missing.

"Remember," Jim said, "honk the horn three times if you see Shirley or Mrs. Ivey coming."

"What're ya gonna do if I have ta honk the horn?"

"I'll run out the front door."

"What about me?"

Mr. Martin twirled his hat faster and faster and kneaded it harder and harder. Jim worried he might actually shred the old thing.

"Just tell them you saw the truck parked here and decided to wait for a ride."

"What'll I tell 'em about the truck bein' here?"

Jim paused for a moment. Mr. Martin was making his plan more complicated than it needed to be.

"Tell them you thought my dad was running an errand and would be right back."

He decided that sounded plausible. His father often parked in that exact spot when he was in town. Of course, it was only when he ate at the café, but Jim didn't think Mr. Martin needed to know that detail.

"Then what?"

"I'll run to the end of the block and wait."

"Then what?"

"I'll come back here when the coast is clear and take you home."

"Don't ya fergit about me."

"Don't worry," he said. "Everything will be fine."

Jim swung the truck door open just far enough to slip out. He wasn't sure the singing coming from the empty lot would cover the noise of closing it. To be safe, he left the door ajar.

He hunched over, ran around to the front of the truck and waited. When he was certain no one was watching him, he ran up the back steps.

He opened the door a few inches and squeezed inside. The last thing he heard before the door closed behind him was Mr. Martin's voice.

"Ya give George a pat on the head fer me."

Twenty-one

All the businesses in Willowdale were closed on Sundays, and I enjoyed the extra hour of sleep. When I woke up, I lay in bed longer than normal, but I couldn't stay there forever.

I threw off my blanket and immediately regretted it. My arm and back muscles screamed in pain from all the raking I did. Every movement was agony.

"You have to get up," I said to myself. "Quit stalling."

I threw my legs over the edge of the mattress and catapulted myself to a seated position. I sat for only a second and forced myself to stand up.

"Ouch."

I shuffled over to the closet and stared at my clothes. After a minute or two, I decided I wasn't ready to change out of my nightgown after all.

I closed the closet door and grabbed my robe off the hook on the wall. I slipped it on, stepped into my moccasins and walked over to the desk.

My daily letter to Dad was in the bottom drawer. After working on the lot and feeding the boys afterward, I had been too tired to finish it.

I gathered up the writing tablet and a pen and crept downstairs—one agonizing step at a time. There weren't any sounds coming from Grandma's bedroom, so I tiptoed to the kitchen.

George was still asleep on his bed, and I tried not to groan when I picked him up. He barely opened his eyes and lay limp in my arms.

I whispered in his ear, "You could help me just a little."

When he didn't move a muscle to help, I pulled him tighter against my chest. I pushed my back against the screen door and used my toe to block it from slamming shut. Somehow, I managed to get to the backyard swing without dropping him or my writing stuff.

"Okay, big guy," I said. "You sleep right here."

I put him on the swing and sat down next to him. Other than the swing, the only movement in the yard was a robin pecking the ground for worms.

"I can't think of a nicer place to sit and finish my letter to Dad," I said. "Can you, George?"

The little dog didn't bother to look at me. He rolled onto his side and let out a deep sigh.

"I know, I know," I said. "Dad passed away a long time ago."

The letters were my special way of keeping a summer diary. No one ever read them, and that was the way I wanted it.

Along with the letters, I kept my savings book in the bottom drawer of the desk. Grandma made me open the account last summer, and I was glad she did. It taught me the value of a dollar.

"Watch your pennies," she said, "and the dimes will take care of themselves."

I did exactly what she said. Every penny I earned at the café was deposited there. Every dime of it was for my college education.

My girlfriends at home were impressed I saved my money, but what they thought wasn't important. Helping Mom pay for my education was.

"By the end of summer, I'll have enough saved to pay for a full year of tuition at Ball State."

The little dog continued to ignore me. He couldn't possibly understand how important that money was to my mother and me.

"It's a big deal, George," I said. "It's actually a really big deal, helping pay for my education."

I laid my pen and writing tablet next to me and reached over to the little pug. I ran my hand up and down the soft hair on his side.

"You're one special dog, big guy."

Dr. Thompson said he was lucky to have survived his cross-country hike from the mill. I didn't think luck had anything to do with it. I truly believed it was a miracle.

"I guess you're just meant to be here with Grandma and me."

My hair hung straight down over my shoulders, and I ran my hand over it. It felt coarse compared to George's hair and looked dull and lifeless compared to Betty's.

She was as beautiful as her aunt with her clear, cream-colored skin. Not like my face with freckles dotted across my nose and cheeks.

"No wonder Jim prefers her over me," I said. "What boy wouldn't?"

It was no use regretting what I couldn't change. I leaned my head against the back of the swing and watched George sleep. A light breeze ruffled the thick mane around his neck.

The slow back and forth motion of the swing was relaxing, but I couldn't fall sleep. Something about George bothered me.

"I don't know, big guy," I said. "Are you putting on a lot of weight?"

He answered me by rolling onto his back and revealing his well-rounded stomach. It didn't make sense. Grandma and I were careful about his food portions.

"Maybe it's my imagination," I said. "I'll ask Grandma what she thinks."

After several minutes of relaxing, the scent of freshly brewed coffee came from the direction of the kitchen. It was Grandma's not-so-subtle signal that she was up and ready to eat breakfast.

"Let's go" I said, nudging George awake. "I'll write my letter tonight."

I picked up the tablet and pen and carried them and George into the house. As soon as I set the little pug on the floor, he pulled away from my grasp and waddled over to his blanket.

"Good morning, dear."

"Good morning, Grandma," I said. "Do you think George is getting fat?"

She looked over at him. With a wave of her hand, she dismissed the idea.

"He looks perfectly fine to me."

She continued setting the kitchen table with her favorite china and linen napkins. Next to the stove were the bacon and eggs she wanted me to cook.

I laid my writing tablet and pen on the table, walked to the sink and washed my hands. Grandma's apron was on the counter. I dried my hands on it and tied it around my waist.

Breakfast on Sunday was team work in action. She made her coffee and set the table, and I fixed the food. Afterward, we both cleared the table and did the dishes.

"I thought we might take a picnic lunch to Lake Sullivan today," Grandma said. "What do you think?"

"We worked hard on the lot yesterday," I said. "I think we earned it."

She smiled, placed her steaming cup of coffee on the table and sat down. I walked to the stove, lined up the bacon in a cast-iron skillet and turned on the gas burner.

"When we finish here," she said, "we'll make up some sandwiches."

"Peanut butter and jelly?"

"Of course."

That was Grandma's specialty, and a picnic at the lake wouldn't be the same without them. If we added potato chips and apples to the menu, our lunch would be complete.

"By the way," she said. "I have invited Mr. Martin to join us."

"Okay, I guess."

I didn't mind taking him with us to the lake once in a while. I just wished I could spend some time alone with Grandma.

When the bacon was brown and crisp, I scooped the slices onto a serving plate. I poured most of the fat left in the skillet into the grease jar beside the stove.

I broke the four eggs into a bowl and added a little milk and butter. After I whipped it all together with a fork, I poured the mixture into the same skillet.

"I don't cook as well as Irene or Aunt Maude," I said, "but we won't starve as long as I can fix breakfast."

Grandma laughed and leaned against the backrest on her chair. She watched me stir the eggs with the fork.

"We make quite a pair, you and I," she said.

"How's that, Grandma?"

"You make the best scrambled eggs this side of the Mississippi River," she said. "I make the best peanut butter and jelly sandwiches this side of Main Street."

Twenty-two

When we got to Lake Sullivan, a posted sign warned us of the county's new rules. Parking was restricted to an official parking lot. No more parking on the beach.

"Ye gods and little fishes," Grandma said. "What is the meaning of this?"

The designated lot was small and filled with a jumble of vehicles parked at odd angles. I didn't see any way to squeeze Grandpa's truck into the mix.

"I guess we can't stay, Grandma."

"Nonsense," she said, pointing in the direction of the beach. "Park over there."

"I don't know," I said. "The sign says we can't."

"We have always parked on the beach, young lady," she said, "and that is where we will park today."

She didn't think the rules applied to her, but I didn't want to break them. Just the very thought made me nervous.

"Okay, Grandma, we'll park on the beach," I said. "If a space opens up in the lot, I'm moving the truck."

Grandma patted my hand and said, "That's fine, dear, if that makes you feel more comfortable."

I inched Grandpa's truck past the new sign and drove onto the sand. In a few yards, I stopped under the same willow tree we parked under last summer.

Ours was the only vehicle on the beach, and I wanted to disappear before anyone saw us. Grandma didn't seem a bit concerned.

"This is the perfect spot," she said.

The beach beyond the tree was packed with people. Some of them huddled under large beach umbrellas. Others lounged on towels or blankets in full sunlight.

There were young children everywhere. They shouted at each other and ran serpentine patterns around the towels and blankets. They kicked up sand onto everything. It was bedlam.

"Where did all these people come from, Grandma?"

"It does appear the lake has become quite popular."

"I best git us a spot," Mr. Martin said.

He opened the passenger door and nearly fell out of the cab. If he hadn't held onto the door handle, he might have landed face first.

"Are you alright, Mr. Martin?" Grandma said.

"Don't ya worry none about me."

He stood up straight and readjusted his fishing hat. Just a few steps from the truck, he claimed a small area of sand under the willow tree. While he stood guard over it, Grandma and I unloaded our gear.

In a few minutes, the three of us had everything arranged in its proper place. Finally, I lifted George out of the cab and lowered him onto the sand.

Instead of lying on the blanket, he wandered to the base of the tree. He scratched a depression in the sand, spun in place three times and plopped down.

"That really looks comfortable, big guy," I said.

Mr. Martin eased onto one of the canvas folding chairs. He kicked off his shoes, peeled off his socks and stuffed them inside the shoes. He leaned back and pulled his fishing hat over his face.

Grandma, dressed in her sundress and straw hat, slipped out of her sandals. She sat down on the edge of the blanket and ran her fingers through the sand.

"Why don't you go for a swim, dear?" she said. "I'll watch you from here."

"I think I will."

I scanned up and down the water's edge for an opening in the crowd. Beyond the hordes of children playing in the shallows, there was room to swim farther out.

"I won't be long," I said.

I stripped off the shirt and shorts I wore over my one piece bathing suit. After I unbuckled my sandals, I laid them beside the blanket.

"Don't go out too far," Grandma said. "The lifeguard is too busy today to save everyone."

"Oh, Grandma," I said. "I'll be just fine."

It was her job to worry about me, but I was a strong swimmer. Everyone in my family was, and not just because we loved to swim. It was because all children in Indiana were expected to know how.

I half ran, half hopped across the blistering sand until I reached the water's edge. Not an easy feat for someone with stiff, achy muscles.

Two small children were building a drip sand castle on the water's edge and temporarily blocked my path. I stepped around their castle and lunged into deeper water just beyond them.

The sudden coolness felt wonderful on my sore muscles. I rolled onto my back and floated with my eyes closed, enjoying the water's undulating motion.

"Well, look who's here."

It was Jim's voice. It was garbled because my ears were underwater, but I would have recognized it anywhere.

I abandoned the idea of ignoring him and enjoying a peaceful swim. I stood up and looked around me. He was standing only a few feet away.

"Are you talking to me?" I said.

"Who else?"

I wanted to say something sarcastic, but he wasn't alone. Betty was on her back, floating next to him with her hand resting on his shoulder.

"I brought Betty to see the lake."

"So I noticed."

She raised her head a little to look over at me. The action caused her feet to sink slightly, and her fingers tightened on Jim's skin.

"Oh, no," she said.

"Lay your head back so your feet stay up," he said.

She did as he instructed, but her fingers didn't relax. I could see she wasn't comfortable in the water.

"Giving lessons?" I said.

"Betty never learned to swim," he said. "I guess her family didn't think it was important."

"That's too bad."

"Yeah."

"Good luck to both of you," I said. "I'm on my way to the floating platform."

I pushed my feet against the bottom of the lake and did a dolphin-like dive. When I surfaced, I swam away from them as fast as I could. I didn't want any part of Betty's swimming lesson.

At the floating platform, I had to tread water and wait in line for the ladder. It seemed all the swimmers decided to practice diving at exactly the same time.

Once it was my turn, I climbed the ladder and looked for a place to sit. I found a narrow open space along the front edge.

I sat down and wiggled more space between the people on either side of me. When I was settled, I scanned the lake between the platform and the shoreline.

The water was frothy with countless swimmers. In the midst of all of that, I saw Betty and Jim.

She was still floating on her back, holding onto Jim's shoulder. He was piloting her around the other swimmers and moving her closer to shore.

"That's probably the shortest swimming lesson in history," I said under my breath.

When they got to shore, Betty stood up and scurried onto the beach. I expected Jim to help her across the sand to a blanket somewhere, but he didn't get out of the water.

"What's he doing?"

He turned sharply and dived into deeper water. When he surfaced, he was halfway to the floating platform.

"Oh, no," I said. "I think he's headed this way."

His strong arms and excellent form got him to the platform in no time. Instead of waiting his turn, I watched him shove his way through the line and propel himself up the ladder. He found where I was sitting and stood over me, dripping water.

"Hey, Shirley."

I wanted to get away from him by jumping off the platform and swimming for shore. But it was a half-baked idea at best. I knew he would jump right in and catch up to me.

"Are you just going to stand there or are you going to sit down?"

"Since you asked," he said, "I think I'll sit down."

I scooted over a little to give him room, and he sat down with a splat. The boy next to him got up and moved to another location.

"I thought you were giving Betty swimming lessons."

"I was."

"How did she do?"

"She got cold."

He infuriated me even more than usual. Why did I have to drag information out of him?

"I mean, how did she do before that?"

"I don't think she likes to swim."

"How do you know?"

"She complained about her face getting wet."

That was funny, and I couldn't stop myself from laughing. Swimming without getting her face wet was one of the dumbest things I'd ever heard.

"It's not that funny, Shirley."

Before I had a chance to say anything more, I heard a clap of thunder. I stopped laughing.

"That can't be right," I said. "Just look how sunny it is."

Jim's head swiveled first to the left and then to the right, his eyes scanning the horizon. I followed his gaze, but I couldn't see where the sound was coming from.

"There," he said, pointing across the lake. "Look behind that line of trees."

He was right. A thunderhead was building, and a rising wind was pushing whitecaps across the lake. Our pleasant day was about to turn ugly.

"Listen to that," I said.

The single clap of thunder became a barrage of rumbles. On shore, the lifeguard blew his whistle in a series of three long blasts. The sound was barely audible against the freshening wind at the platform.

I looked at Jim, and he looked at me. Nothing needed to be said. I knew I needed to postpone any angry feelings I had.

"We have to get these people off the platform, Shirley."

"What are we waiting for?"

We both jumped to our feet and yelled at everyone. We urged them to get into the water and head to safety.

Some of them jumped or dived into the water and swam for the shore. Others stood transfixed at the sight of the looming cloud.

"If we have to force them into the water," Jim said, "that's what we'll do."

He ran to the opposite side of the platform. I turned toward a young girl standing next to me.

She was paralyzed in the midst of all the commotion. Her face was pale, and her arms were wrapped across her chest. She was shivering uncontrollably.

"We're going to jump into the water now," I said.

"I—can't."

"Yes, you can," I said. "We're going to swim back to shore together."

"You won't leave me?"

"Absolutely not."

She looked up at me with her wide brown eyes. Getting her back to shore became my top priority.

"Take my hand," I said.

She did as she was told, but her fingers were ice-cold. If I didn't get her to shore soon, I was afraid she would go into shock.

"What's your name?"

"Cin—dy."

"My name is Shirley."

She only nodded. Her frightened expression told me the rest of the story.

"How old are you?"

"I'm—eight."

I had her full attention, but I needed to hurry. I squeezed her hand a little tighter and lead her to the edge of the platform.

"Okay, Cindy," I said. "I'll count to three, and we'll jump into the water together."

"Okay."

"One, two, three—jump!"

As we fell toward the choppy water, I thought about Grandma and George and Mr. Martin. I couldn't be on shore to help them. All I could do was hope and pray they found shelter in the truck.

Twenty-three

The worst of the storm was over, but there was still a steady rain. I moved the wiper lever on Grandpa's old truck back and forth, trying to keep the windshield clear. To keep it from fogging, I cranked the bottom of it open a little.

The temperature had dropped several degrees, and the cab was cold and damp. I switched on the blower and turned the hot water valve all the way open.

Mr. Martin reached down and opened the doors on the heater box by his feet. There wasn't much heat blowing out of the box, but it was better than nothing.

"Are you feeling any better, dear?"

"I'm okay, Grandma."

Actually, I was chilled to the bone and couldn't stop shivering. I had spent too much time in the lake, but it couldn't be avoided.

The lifeguard was overwhelmed by the number of swimmers, and Jim and I did our best to help. I lost count how many times I swam back and forth between the platform and the shore. Finally, the three of us pushed or pulled every frightened swimmer to safety.

Not only was I cold, I was exhausted. I didn't have the energy to drive, but I had no choice. Grandma didn't know how to drive, Mr. Martin couldn't see and George was—a dog. He was sitting on Grandma's lap and staring out the windshield.

"You were very brave today," Grandma said. "You saved a great many lives."

She reached up and put her hand on my shoulder. I felt the warmth of her touch through the beach towel, but it wasn't enough to warm me.

"Thanks, Grandma," I said. "I hope I helped a little."

"Oh, my dear, that was more than a little help."

I was too cold and too tired to think about it anymore. I wanted to go home and take a hot bath, but Grandma insisted we drive into town.

When we turned onto Main Street, I understood why. There was only one empty parking space the full length of the street. It was directly in front of the café.

"Just as I suspected," Grandma said. "We have a few customers."

That was an enormous understatement. I couldn't believe how many cars and trucks were parked on both sides of the street. Some I recognized, but most were new to me.

"You were right, Grandma," I said. "Everybody came to the café."

"Of course," she said. "This is where they always come after an emergency."

I parked the truck in the empty space and pulled the towel tighter around my shoulders. I picked up George and my dry sandals and clothes.

"You and Mr. Martin go first, Grandma."

I waited until they were out of the truck and under shelter of the café's awning. In spite of my tired muscles, I slipped out of the cab and made a run for it. Not easy with an overweight pug in my arms.

"You folks get yourselves in here right now," Irene said.

She stood at the front door, holding it open for us. Once we were all inside, she slammed the door closed behind us.

"Thank you, Irene, for coming and getting everything started," Grandma said.

"I only live a couple of blocks away, you know," she said. "I figured everybody'd be headed here."

She was right. The dining room was packed, and it sounded as though everyone was speaking at once.

Grandma and Irene elbowed their way through the crowd, and George and I followed behind them. When we got to the back of the café, they stopped in the kitchen. George and I went straight to the game room.

Two young children were playing a heated game of checkers. I ignored them and laid George on his bed.

There were still a few embers at the back of the potbellied stove. I opened the door and tossed a handful of kindling on top of them. While I waited for them to catch, I sat next to George and dried my hair.

In a minute or two, the kindling burst into flames and ignited a log left from the last fire. The sudden warmth felt good, but it wasn't enough to take away my chill. I needed to change into something warmer than my wet bathing suit.

"You stay here, George."

I didn't have to worry about that. He was already asleep, but he was curled into a ball, shivering. I draped my towel across his back and tucked it in around him.

I closed the door on the stove, gave him a quick kiss on the top of his head and stood up. With my dry clothes and sandals in hand, I went to the small bathroom to change.

While I switched out of my suit, I heard Grandma's voice over the din in the dining room. She was greeting customers as they arrived and making sure everyone had something hot to drink.

"It doesn't look like there's any damage in Willowdale," one woman said.

"Wait until tomorrow morning," Grandma said. "When the farmers come for breakfast, they will tell us about any damage in the county."

"How do they know?" another woman said.

"Farmers are always the first to know details about the crops and buildings," Grandma said.

After I finished dressing and tying a new ponytail, I went back to the dining room. I was surprised at how many more survivors of the storm had arrived.

"Wow," I said to myself. "Everyone in the whole county must be here."

Every chair was taken, including Grandpa's, but Grandma didn't appear concerned about that. She continued to greet new arrivals and make sure they had a place to sit.

When she saw me, she gave me one of her stern looks. I couldn't imagine what that was about until she nodded in my direction.

"My granddaughter," she said, "will be happy to serve you more coffee and hot chocolate."

I took the hint, turned around and went to the kitchen. Irene was at the stove stirring hot milk with a wooden spoon. She looked up at me and sighed.

"Those folks out there sure are a thirsty bunch," she said.

"Grandma wants me to serve them some more."

She smiled at me and went back to making the new pot of hot chocolate. I washed my hands at the sink and slipped on a clean bib apron.

"It looks like they plan on staying until the rain stops," I said.

"Sure does," Irene said. "Your grandma's lovin' every minute of it."

I picked up a carafe of coffee in one hand and a pot of hot chocolate in the other. I went back into the dining room and wandered from table to table, refilling empty cups.

Grandma was at the front of the café. She was arranging a cushion on top of the radiator as a makeshift seat. When I passed by her, she grinned at me.

"Ye gods," she said. "Willowdale hasn't had this much excitement since last summer."

"It's mighty hospitable of you to take us all in this way," a woman at the counter said.

"It is our pleasure," Grandma said.

While I poured cup after cup of coffee and hot chocolate, Grandma wandered the room. She stopped at every table and chatted with every customer.

"That's Mrs. Ivey for you," Mr. Wilson said to the woman at the counter. "She won't let you leave cold or hungry."

I didn't mean to eavesdrop, but I couldn't help but overhear them. It was the nicest thing I ever heard, and I was glad he appreciated Grandma's generosity. I wished the two people sitting at the back of the room felt the same way.

Miss Carter and Betty were huddled together at one of the small tables. Jim sat across them. He was still wearing his swim trunks, and a beach towel was around his shoulders.

I didn't want to deal with Betty and her aunt, but they were customers, too. I let out a heavy sigh and forced myself to walk over to their table.

"Would anyone like more to drink?" I said.

Betty smiled and held up her cup for me to refill with hot chocolate. Jim kept his hands wrapped around a cup of coffee, and Miss Carter stared at me.

Jim's hair was still wet, and he was shivering. Miss Carter and Betty, on the other hand, looked comfortable in their stylish raincoats.

I ignored Betty's request for more hot chocolate. Instead, I concentrated on Jim's blue lips and drooping eyelids.

"Remember Grandpa's old clothes he left here in case of emergencies, Jim?"

"Yeah," he said. "I remember."

"Well, they're still here."

"Okay."

"You're welcome to get out of your wet things and put them on."

"Okay."

Even though his hands were wrapped around a steaming cup, his teeth chattered. The drink wasn't warming him, and I was afraid he was on the verge of hypothermia.

"Alright, Jim, that's not a suggestion anymore," I said. "That's an order."

"You can't come back here and order him around," Betty said.

She glared at me, and I thought she was going to jump up and hit me. I knew she was self-centered, but I never imagined she was uncaring, too.

"This isn't about you or me, Betty," I said. "Jim needs dry clothes."

"Now, Shirley, I am certain Jim knows what is best for himself," Miss Carter said.

Jim looked at Betty and then at her aunt. Without a word to either of them, he pushed his chair away from the table and stood up.

"What are you doing?" Betty said.

"I'm taking the advice of a friend," he said.

His words were a little slurred and barely audible, but the message was clear. With no more explanation than that, he walked away from the table and followed me to the back of the café.

"It's okay if I call you my friend, isn't it?" he said.

"We'll talk about that later," I said. "Grandpa's old clothes are in the cupboard behind the bathroom door."

"Thanks, Shirley."

I dropped off the coffee and hot chocolate in the kitchen. I planned to refill the two pots after I checked on George.

Grandma was in the game room, supervising a game of Chinese checkers between two young boys. She looked up at me when I walked into the room.

"Shirley, dear," she said. "I would like to point out something to you."

She left the two boys with their game and led me to the chair next to George's bed. The little pug was still asleep, but he was no longer shivering.

"What is it, Grandma?"

"Look at the floor and tell me what you see."

I scanned the floor around George's bed and the easy chair. I noticed small pieces of debris.

I reached down, picked up several of the pieces and rolled them between my fingers. They were bits of chaff like the kind I saw at Mr. Spencer's mill.

"Mr. Martin swept in here yesterday after the café closed," I said. "Could he have missed these?"

"That's just it," Grandma said. "He is too meticulous to have missed them."

I looked over at her, and studied her face. Did she think I somehow tracked them in on my shoes?

"What are you thinking, Grandma?"

"I believe someone was in here while we were busy in the empty lot."

"George was in here by himself that whole time."

I turned to look into the dining room, hoping to find the answer there. All I saw was Jim standing in the game room doorway wearing Grandpa's clothes.

"Thank you for lending me Mr. Ivey's things," he said.

"Ye gods," Grandma said with a wave of her hand. "After all your hard work at the lake, it is the least I can do."

Grandpa had been a tall man, and his clothes were way too large. With the pant legs and the shirt sleeves rolled up, they fit Jim well enough. At least his tennis shoes were dry so he didn't have to wear Grandpa's shoes.

"I'll bring everything back tomorrow," he said. "Right after I sweep up the mill."

I looked at Grandma, and she looked at me. We both looked back at Jim.

"Don't worry," he said. "I'll be a mess, but I promise Mr. Ivey's clothes will be clean."

"I'm not a bit concerned about that," Grandma said.

I was happy to see his lips weren't blue anymore. His hair was nearly dry, too, and he wasn't shivering.

"Thanks, again," he said.

He wrapped his wet swim trunks inside his towel and walked back into the dining room. Grandma and I watched him until he went out of sight behind the back wall.

"Are you thinking what I'm thinking, Grandma?"

We both turned around and looked at George. He was on his side, and it was easy to see his expanding waistline.

"I believe we have solved our little mystery, dear."

Twenty-four

"Such a glorious day with not a cloud in the sky," Elaine said. "One would never know there was a storm yesterday."

She stood with her niece at the front window and watched cars and trucks pass by. Two trucks were parked in front of Ivey's Café. The spaces in front of her coffee shop remained empty.

"I simply do not understand," she said. "We have been open for two hours. Not one of my usual customers has stopped in."

"Where could they be?" Betty said.

"I have no idea," she said. "Thankfully, Marie is only slightly busier than we are."

"At least she has customers."

Elaine looked at her niece. She wondered if the girl truly didn't understand the situation.

"The point is," she said, "why does she have any business at all?"

"Maybe when Jim gets here, he can tell us what's going on."

"Perhaps he can," she said. "However, I am quite disappointed with that boy at the moment."

"Why, Aunt Elaine?"

"You haven't forgotten how rudely he behaved toward us at the café yesterday, have you?"

"I remember he was being manipulated by Shirley."

"Isn't that boy old enough to have a mind of his own?"

"Of course, he is," Betty said. "Shirley just took advantage of the whole storm situation."

"I hope he remembers where his loyalties lie."

"His loyalties, Aunt Elaine?"

"He works for me, Betty," she said. "I expect him to honor that arrangement at all times."

Elaine turned away from the window. She roamed around the coffee shop, straightening chairs and fluffing pillows. At one of the floor-to-ceiling bookcases, she discovered two books out of order.

"Do you remember I want all the books displayed alphabetically by the author's last name?"

Betty was nearly halfway to the gift shop. She stopped short and turned around.

"Yes, I remember, Aunt Elaine."

"I want you to spend this free time by inventorying all the books," she said. "Make certain they are displayed properly."

"Yes, Aunt Elaine."

Betty walked over to the first bookcase, but Elaine's attention was drawn to the coffee table. Books left by one of her customers were stacked on it. She couldn't imagine her niece didn't notice them.

"I suggest you begin by organizing the books scattered about the room."

"I thought your customers would want me to leave the books where they are."

"Why would you think that?"

"I thought they might come back later and finish reading them."

"That won't do," she said. "My customers know they are to return their books to the proper shelves before they leave."

Betty walked over to the coffee table. Instead of collecting the entire stack, she picked up one book. She returned it to its shelf and walked back to the table for another one.

Her inefficient method grated on Elaine's nerves, but her mind was on more important matters. She went to the front of the room and looked out the window.

"I see the boys are at work on the empty lot again," she said.

"Every day they do a little more, Aunt Elaine."

"Have you any idea what that is all about?"

Her niece restacked the book she was holding before joining her at the window. They stood side by side and watched the work in progress across the street.

"The lot really looks better, don't you think?" Betty said.

"The fact it looks better is all well and good," Elaine said. "The real conundrum is why Marie is cleaning it after so many years of neglect."

"I see what you mean."

"Good," she said. "You can glean that information from Jim if and when he arrives."

"He promised he'd be here after he finishes helping his father."

"I certainly hope so," she said. "We need that boy to keep us informed."

Twenty-five

I was replacing old newspapers with new ones when I heard the back door open and close. I expected to see Mr. Martin come into the dining room, but he didn't.

The only other people in the cafe were two farmers sitting at the lunch counter. Unlike most mornings, they weren't discussing the weather or the price of crops. They weren't talking at all.

"Can I get you some more coffee?" I said.

"Whenever you got time," one of them said.

"Yeah, whenever," the other one said.

Whenever I have time? Since when did they care about my time? They usually groused about how long it took to get a refill.

Since I was going to the kitchen for coffee anyway, I bundled up the old papers. I carried them to the back door for Mr. Martin to put in Grandpa's truck.

I was about to drop the bundle on the floor when I noticed a trail of debris. It led from the back door to the game room.

"What—?"

Irene was in the kitchen, stirring pots and chopping food. I was pretty sure no one could hear me over all that noise.

Just to be sure, I lowered the papers to the floor without a sound. If someone were in the game room, I didn't want him to know I was there.

"Whoever you are," I whispered, "you're going to have to deal with me."

I tiptoed to the game room door and stopped with my back to the wall. I peeked around the door frame looking for the intruder. I found him.

Jim was sitting on the floor next to George. He was covered in debris from his baseball cap to the soles of his tennis shoes. He held something wrapped in waxed paper. George stared up at him and wagged his tail until his whole body wiggled.

"Sorry there isn't more for you today," he said. "We didn't have many leftovers in the house."

He tore open the paper and fed small pieces of meat to George. Every time Jim offered him a bite, the little pug leaned forward and snatched it from his fingers.

They were completely engrossed with each other. Neither of them noticed me.

"Don't you tell anybody I was here, okay?" Jim said. "I'd be in more trouble if they knew."

I couldn't believe my eyes or my ears. No wonder our little boy was gaining weight.

"I can't stay long this time," he said. "I have to get over to the coffee shop."

He stuffed the empty waxed paper in his pocket, straightened the wrinkles out of George's blanket and gave the little dog a long hug. When he stood up, George settled down on the blanket and licked his front feet.

I should have jumped out from my hiding place and con- fronted Jim. Something stopped me.

Maybe it was a lapse in judgement or temporary insanity. Whatever it was, I felt sorry for him and didn't want to spoil the moment.

At the front of the café, I heard Grandma come through the door. She was with the latest group of boys helping to clear the empty lot.

"You boys go sit at the table," she said.

Jim looked up in the direction of the dining room. I jumped back behind the door frame before he saw me.

"I have to go now," Jim said. "You be a good boy until I come back."

Since I didn't want Jim to know I was there, I tiptoed to the bathroom and hid inside. I listened to the squeak of his tennis shoes on the polished floor as he went by. When I heard the back door close, I knew he was gone.

"I wonder—"

I opened the cupboard behind the bathroom door. There were Grandpa's clothes just as Jim promised. They were clean and neatly folded on the bottom shelf.

"That's one point in your favor, Jim."

I left my hiding place, took one last look at George and hurried to the kitchen. I grabbed a pot of coffee off the stove.

Irene was at the cutting board beside the sink, chopping green peppers and smelly onions. Hamburger was browning in a Dutch oven for the day's chili special. My mouth watered and my stomach growled.

"That sure was some storm," Irene said, dabbing at tears with the hem of her apron.

"It sure was," I said. "Everybody told me how much they enjoyed your coffee and hot chocolate."

"That's real kind of you to say so."

I heard Grandma tell the boys to help themselves to the sandwiches Irene made for them. Chairs scraped against the floor, and Grandma's shoes clicked in the direction of the lunch counter.

"How are you men today?" she said.

The farmers began talking all at once about the storm damage to their properties. I didn't want to miss a word, so I hurried into the dining room with the coffee.

"At least we didn't get any hail," one of them said.

"But Pete's pole barn needs a new roof."

"And my Lizzy's laundry blew clean off the clothesline."

"It really is a shame about Pete," Grandma said. "I'm certain he could use some help repairing the roof."

As usual, Grandma was a good sounding board for them. I felt sorry for Lizzy and sympathized about Pete's barn. I was just afraid their conversation would go on forever.

I didn't have time for that if the lot project was going to get finished. I needed to keep my volunteers focused on the job at hand.

I walked over to the front table where the boys were sitting and stared at them. They stopped eating and looked up at me.

"Get done with your sandwiches," I said. "I'll be waiting outside for you."

I was getting used to being in charge and didn't give them a chance to argue. I walked to the counter, poured the farmers their refills and set the pot down.

I didn't say anything to them or to Grandma. I walked back past the boys and out the front door.

Across the street, the huge "Elaine's" sign with its gaudy floral border seemed to stare at me. The hideous thing stirred up my teenage anger. I lost my patience, and I didn't wait another minute for the boys.

I poked my head inside the café door. Grandma and the farmers were still discussing the condition of Pete's roof. In order for the boys to hear me, I had to shout over their voices.

"Put down those sandwiches and get out here," I said. "It's time to go back to work."

Twenty-six

"I'm telling you, Miss Carter," Jim said. "No one knows why Mrs. Ivey is cleaning up the empty lot."

"She must have said something about it to someone."

Elaine looked directly into Jim's eyes. She couldn't be certain he was telling her everything.

"There must be someone besides Shirley in whom she confides."

"I don't know who that would be," he said. "Even Mr. Martin says he doesn't have any idea."

"What about Pastor Lawrence?" she said. "He and Mrs. Ivey appear to be good friends."

"He's never said anything about it to me."

She sat forward on the sofa across from Jim and Betty and sipped her herbal tea. She didn't know what to believe. The boy's loyalty was questionable after he was so easily manipulated by Shirley after the storm.

"From what I saw at the café yesterday," she said, "it appears you and Shirley resolved whatever issues you had with one another."

Jim drank from his mug of hot chocolate and avoided eye contact with her. He squirmed a little in his chair, and looked over at Betty.

"I hope Shirley and I can be friends again someday," he said. "She's a really nice girl."

Betty's bottom lip quivered, and tears welled up in her eyes. Elaine was disgusted to see her niece was so weak. Didn't she understand how much power a woman could wield over a man?

"There is no need for tears, Betty," she said. "Here, take this."

She unpinned a handkerchief from the front of her dress and handed it to her niece. Betty wiped her eyes with the lacy square of fabric and blew her nose. Elaine cringed at the very thought of her favorite French hankie being defiled.

"You may launder that before you return it."

"Yes, Aunt Elaine."

Jim put his mug on the coffee table and slouched into the overstuffed chair. His shoes and clothes were dotted with pieces of grain. Elaine wondered how many minutes it would take to shake out the slipcover once he was gone.

"Perhaps you can tell us why Mrs. Ivey has customers this morning and we don't."

"That one's easy," he said. "The café is where the farmers always go to give updates after a storm."

"Wouldn't they visit all the businesses to inform everyone individually?"

Jim sat up and scooted to the edge of the chair. Elaine couldn't read his expression.

"They talk to Mrs. Ivey because they like her, and they respect her opinion about everything."

"I have opinions, too."

"Sure, Miss Carter," Jim said, "but you're too new to this town."

"What do you mean by that, young man?"

Jim stood up and looked down at her. He slapped his baseball cap against his pant leg, sending dust flying everywhere. He slipped the cap on his head and turned toward the front door.

"You have to earn Willowdale's respect, Miss Carter," he said. "Until then, you'll always be an outsider."

Elaine put down her cup and jumped to her feet. She had never been spoken to in such a manner. She wasn't about to allow someone like Jim Spencer to speak to her with such disrespect. Outsider was she?

"I don't appreciate your attitude," she said.

"You can take it or leave it," Jim said. "This is a small town, and it takes us a long time to trust newcomers."

Elaine stepped in front of Jim and stared him in the eye. She wasn't about to endure anymore rudeness from her niece's latest fling.

"Our association has come to an end, young man," she said, "and you are no longer welcome to socialize with my niece."

"Aunt Elaine!"

Betty bolted from her chair, ran to Jim's side and slipped her hands around his arm. Tears streamed down her cheeks.

"Please, Jim, tell Aunt Elaine you're sorry for making her mad."

"I make no apologies," he said. "I only speak the truth."

Elaine pried her niece's hands from Jim's arm and shoved her away. She wondered if Betty had any shame at all, acting that way around a boy.

"You have just confirmed what I have been saying about you all along," Elaine said.

Jim walked to the front door and pulled it open. When he turned around, his face was flushed.

"What exactly have you been saying about me all along, Miss Carter?"

"You are an unsuitable companion for my beautiful and well-bred niece."

"Well, you don't have to worry about that anymore," he said.

"What are you saying, Jim?" Betty said, wiping at her tears with the cuff of her blouse.

"You don't have to fire me, Miss Carter," he said. "I don't hang around anywhere I'm not wanted."

He let the door slam closed behind him, and Elaine winced at the sound. His behavior was inexcusable. She was relieved the ill-mannered boy was gone from her employment and from her niece's life.

"Well," Betty said. "Good riddance."

She fell back onto an easy chair and crossed her arms in front of her chest. She glared at the closed door.

Elaine shook her head at her niece's childish antics, but breathed a sigh of relief. It appeared to have only taken her a few seconds to dismiss Jim from her life. She just hoped Betty wasn't putting on an act for her benefit.

"There are many fine young men, Betty," she said. "Someday, one of them will meet with our approval."

"Yes, Aunt Elaine."

"For now," she said, "you and I must formulate a new plan to lure back our customers."

"Yes, Aunt Elaine."

Twenty-seven

The second group of boys from the church choir worked as hard as the first group. The empty lot finally lived up to its name.

The weeds were cut down and the overgrown grass was mowed. The old pop bottles and newspapers were in gunny sacks and ready to be delivered to the dump. There was nothing but a clean slate for my design of Grandma's patio.

"It's perfect," I said to myself.

The boys had gone home, and Grandma was still inside discussing storm damage with the farmers. Since I was the only one left on the job site, I had no choice but to talk to myself.

"Let's see," I said. "The window over there will be replaced by a door, and we'll need at least a couple of steps built."

My plan seemed a lot simpler when it was only a drawing on a piece of paper. With the work actually started, I had no idea who would do the construction.

Even if I found a contractor and the materials I needed, I still had a problem. How was I going pay for it all?

"Grandma, you must have a whole lot of faith in me."

In my hands I held a ball of string I found in Grandma's kitchen drawer. The front pockets on my jeans were full of large nails from Grandpa's workbench in the garage.

My plan was to use the string to outline the area where I wanted the patio built. The nails were to secure the string to the ground.

I looked all around me for a big rock. The boys did such a good job, there wasn't one rock large enough to use as a hammer.

"How could I be so stupid," I said. "I could have brought one of Grandpa's hammers."

"Well, Shirley, that'll teach you to be better prepared next time."

It was Jim's voice. I whipped myself around, stumbling over my own feet. He was only a couple of yards from me. His hands were in his pockets, and he had a silly grin on his face.

"How long have you been standing there?"

"Don't worry," he said. "I won't tell anybody you talk to yourself."

"Thanks, I think."

My cheeks felt so warm, I was sure I was blushing. Not even the straw hat could hide that from him.

"What are you doing here anyway?" I said.

"I saw you out here by yourself and thought you could use an extra hand."

"Up until a few minutes ago, I had lots of help."

"What did you do, scare them away?"

Why did he have to be so infuriating? I knew he was joking, but I wasn't in the mood for it. I still had a lot to do before Grandma and I left for home.

"All my helpers had to go home and do chores, if you must know."

"Easy," he said, raising one hand. "I didn't mean to make you mad."

I adjusted my hat so I could see him better. He was wearing the same shirt and pants he wore when he sneaked in to see George.

"Aren't you supposed to be running errands or something for Miss Carter?"

"Nope," he said. "I don't work for her anymore."

My mouth dropped open, and I stared at him. I never expected to hear him say that.

"What happened?" I said.

"Let's just say Miss Carter doesn't like to hear the truth."

"The truth about what?"

"Life."

"Do you mean anything in particular about life or just life in general?"

"I'd say it's more like life in Willowdale."

That narrowed it down a little, but I knew Jim. He wasn't about to say anything more no matter how much I pried.

"If you don't mind," I said. "I have to get back to work."

I tucked the ball of string under my arm and dug into my jeans pockets with both hands. I retrieved all the nails and handed them to Jim.

"What am I supposed to do with these?" he said.

"Can you find a big rock?" I said.

"I suppose."

"You might need one to get those into the ground."

Jim pushed his baseball cap higher on his forehead. He looked confused, and I struggled to keep from laughing at him.

"Why would I want to put these in the ground?"

"Because," I said, "you're going to help me mark where the patio will be."

"What patio?"

"Just follow me, and I'll show you."

I led him to the side of the building and placed my hand on the brick. Just the idea of sharing my plan with Jim made me feel less overwhelmed.

"This is where the door will go," I said.

"Okay."

"The patio will be right where we're standing."

"Okay."

"There will be shade trees all around the edge of the patio to keep the sun off the customers."

"Wait a second," he said. "What are the customers doing out here?"

"Eating," I said. "Did I forget to mention the tables and chairs?"

"Yeah, you did."

"There's one big problem," I said.

"Just one?"

"Do you know anyone who can put in a door where the window is and build a couple of steps?"

Jim backed up a little and scanned the side of the building. He stepped off a measurement along the wall and shoved a nail into the ground. I couldn't believe he did it with his bare hands.

"This is where you should start your patio," he said. "How big do you want it?"

It was the first time anyone asked me that. I had no idea how much room it would take.

"I'll need enough room for five or six tables."

"What about room for all the chairs?"

"Oh, yeah," I said. "Each table should have four chairs."

Jim paced off one side of the proposed patio area and pushed another nail into the ground. After he measured the other two sides, he left a nail at each corner.

"How's that look?" he said. "I figure it's enough space for six tables with four chairs each."

I stood in the center of the rectangle and marveled at the size of it. I didn't realize it would occupy such a large portion of the lot.

"Let me run the string around the nails and see how it feels," I said.

It only took me a few minutes to outline the patio. When I was done, the project felt even more real.

"Have you thought about dogs?" Jim said.

"What about dogs?"

"Half the people in town allow their dogs to run loose," he said.

"Yeah?"

"How are you going to keep them off the patio?"

The project was getting so complicated my head hurt. I wondered what else I was forgetting.

"Do you have any ideas about keeping them off?" I said.

"Yep, I do."

I was mentally exhausted and needed to sit down. There was a patch of grass in the center of the rectangle marked by the string. I sat down on it.

"If you put up a fence around the perimeter of the patio," he said, "dogs can't get in."

"That makes sense."

"And customers can't get out without paying their bills."

Could the plan get any more complicated? I didn't have money for the door, the steps, the tables and chairs, the limestone pavers or the trees. How was I supposed to pay for a fence?

"That sounds like a good idea, Jim."

"Thanks."

"Do you know anybody who's willing to work without pay and donate all the materials?" I said.

Jim laughed a little and sat down on the bare dirt beside me. We studied the layout of the patio and the proposed location of the door and steps.

"I just might know somebody with lots of friends who would probably work for meals," he said.

"Wow, that's great, Jim."

"The guy might be able to come up with the materials, too, on one condition."

"Oh, sure," I said. "There's always a condition."

Jim turned toward me. He looked as serious as he did when we pulled struggling swimmers to shore during the storm.

"The guy wants to spend some time with George," he said.

Twenty-eight

"Do you see that, Aunt Elaine?"

Her niece was at the front window of the shop pointing at something across the street. She couldn't imagine what Betty found so fascinating about a group of farm boys raking weeds.

"I'm quite certain they will be finished with that project soon," she said. "There is no need to dwell on it."

"It isn't the boys I'm talking about."

Elaine placed her cup of tea on the table. She didn't understand why Betty allowed the work on the lot to consume so much of her attention.

She joined Betty at the window and understood immediately what concerned her niece. It wasn't at all what she expected.

"See what I mean?" Betty said.

Jim and Shirley were seated on the ground in the empty lot, practically shoulder to shoulder. They were laughing and pointing in all directions. For some reason, there were lengths of string staked to the ground.

"I am absolutely shocked," Elaine said. "Why would Mrs. Ivey allow her granddaughter to sit out there with a boy unchaperoned?"

"Jim didn't waste any time forgetting about me, did he?"

"It appears he did not."

As repulsive as it was to her, Elaine was pleased to take advantage of the situation. It was the perfect opportunity to instruct Betty in the proper behavior expected of a Carter woman.

"Consider this incident a learning experience," she said.

"What have I learned?"

"You have learned no proper young lady in our family would act in such a manner."

"No, Aunt Elaine."

"You have also learned no young man worthy of my niece would encourage it."

"No, Aunt Elaine."

"Good girl," she said. "Now, we need to get back to work."

Elaine took Betty's hand and led her to the coffee table. She waited for her niece to sit down before giving her instructions for the new project.

"Your hand writing is lovely, and you have an excellent eye for color," she said.

"Thank you."

"I want you to look through these designs," she said. "Choose the ones you prefer and copy them onto this craft paper."

Betty pulled the designs, a variety of colorful pencils and the craft paper closer to her. She shuffled through the designs and divided them into two stacks.

"These designs won't do," she said.

She pushed that pile away and pulled the second one closer. She examined the designs and chose two.

"These are pretty good, Aunt Elaine," she said. "Did you draw them?"

"I did indeed."

"Why am I copying them?"

Elaine sat down on the sofa on the other side of the table. She needed to explain her new strategy in terms her niece could understand.

"They will be window signs," she said. "It's my next business campaign to compete with Mrs. Ivey."

"I think these will work."

"That's fine," she said. "When you have finished copying the designs, you may add this wording."

"Yes, Aunt Elaine."

She pulled a slip of paper from her dress pocket and handed it to her niece. She had carefully crafted the words to draw customers' attention away from the café.

"This shouldn't take me too long," Betty said.

"Good," she said. "The first sign goes up tomorrow morning."

Elaine was fascinated at how quickly Betty put the incident across the street from her mind. Perhaps working on the signs was exactly what was needed to distract her from thoughts of Jim.

Twenty-nine

"It's July fourth, George," I said. "Do you remember what that means?"

I was at the kitchen table, and the little pug stood next to my chair. He wagged his tail and cocked his head to one side.

"I don't think Grandma remembers either."

She didn't say anything about my birthday before she went to bed. I couldn't blame her if she forgot. She was too busy staying one step ahead of Miss Carter.

Last summer, the whole town threw me a surprise birthday party at the annual community potluck. It was something I would never forget, and I was sure no one else would either.

"It won't be like that this year, big guy," I said. "There's no party, and there're no fireworks."

George stared up at me with his big, round eyes. I already fed him his breakfast, but that didn't stop him from begging for more.

"Sorry," I said. "No more breakfast and no roast beef scraps."

I looked over at the wall clock. Even though the café was closed for the holiday, I was up earlier than usual. There was something important I needed to do, and I was anxious to get started.

The little pug didn't seem to be in any hurry to start the day. He eased onto his stomach, rolled over and waited for his morning tummy rub. I was happy to oblige.

Grandma's bedroom door opened, and she came into the kitchen wearing her blue sundress and sandals. In her hands was a box wrapped in silver paper and topped with a red bow. She laid it on the table in front of me.

"Good morning, Shirley," she said. "Happy birthday."

My mouth dropped open, and my eyes filled with tears. I wasn't expecting a gift.

"Grandma, you remembered."

"How could I possibly forget my favorite granddaughter's birthday?"

"Oh, Grandma," I said. "I'm your only granddaughter."

"That just makes you even more special."

I turned the package over and over, but I couldn't guess what was inside. I really didn't need anything.

"Seventeen," Grandma said. "Can you imagine that?"

I put the package close to the floor so George could sniff it. I was afraid he might think it was food, so I didn't let him sniff very long.

"I don't believe our little boy would be very interested in the contents, dear."

Grandma sat down across from me, and I carefully removed the bow and the tape. I didn't want to tear the paper. Grandma saved bows and wrapping paper to reuse another day.

"Grandma," I said. "They're beautiful."

I held up the Bermuda shorts so we could both admire them. They were made of plaid madras, and the bottoms of the legs were cuffed.

"I felt it was time for you to retire your old paint shorts," she said. "I understand madras is all the fashion these days."

"Thank you so much."

I got up, gave Grandma a big hug and ran upstairs. I changed into my new shorts, my favorite blouse and a pair of white sandals.

In spite of my freckles and dull hair, I felt pretty and loved. I couldn't stop smiling at my reflection in the dresser mirror.

When I got back downstairs, the picnic basket was on the table, and I looked inside. Grandma had packed it with peanut butter and jelly sandwiches, two bottles of pop, a bag of potato chips and four apples. She even included one of George's bowls and a quart jar of water.

"It wouldn't be July fourth without a picnic," she said. "I thought we could have one for breakfast."

"I don't know any rule that says we have to have bacon and eggs."

We both laughed, and George spun in tight circles by the back door. I picked him up, gave him a hug and kissed him on the top of his head. Grandma grabbed the picnic basket and held the door open for George and me.

We piled into the truck, but I didn't ask Grandma where our outing should begin. I already had a destination in mind. I started the engine and headed to town.

"There's one stop we need to make," I said.

When we got to the café, Grandma unlocked the door, and all three of us went inside. She watched as I went to the back of the lunch counter and found Grandpa's old wooden box.

I placed it on the counter and opened the lid. Underneath a layer of white tissue paper was his cherished American flag. I unfolded it until I found the grommets along its edge.

"I promised I would never forget, Grandma," I said, "and I always keep my promises."

We walked outside to the wooden dowel attached to the bricks beside the front door. One by one, I slipped a grommet over each hook along the rod. I brushed out the wrinkles in the cotton material and made sure the stripes hung straight.

"Thank you, Shirley," Grandma said. "Your grandfather would be proud."

"As long as I'm in Willowdale on the fourth," I said, "it will be my honor to put up his flag."

Grandma put her arm around my waist, and I rested my arm across her shoulders. The flag represented the sacrifices our family endured for our country. As long as I lived, none of our relatives who gave their lives would ever be forgotten.

After a few minutes, we went inside, and I put the wooden box back under the counter. George was asleep on his bed in the game room.

"Oh, no, big guy," I said. "This is a day for a picnic, not a nap."

I picked him up. He snuggled up to me and relaxed his full weight against my chest. He was definitely going on a diet.

After we locked up the café, the three of us drove around the countryside looking for a good picnic spot. We found one on the bank of Willow Creek within sight of Mr. Spencer's mill. In the shade of a massive maple tree, we ate our picnic breakfast to the gurgling sound of the water.

"I hope you aren't too disappointed you're not having a party this year."

"Grandma," I said. "On a scale from one to ten, this day is an eleven."

"There is one thing missing, I'm afraid."

"What's that?"

"There isn't a cake," she said. "However, there is some of Irene's fudge sauce in the cooler at the café."

"Is there vanilla ice cream?"

"Of course."

With ice cream and hot fudge on our minds, we had the truck packed in no time. I took us on the most direct route back to town.

When we got to the café, Grandma and I went straight to the kitchen. George went straight to the game room and continued his nap I interrupted.

"I'll get the bowls and the ice cream," Grandma said. "You heat up the fudge."

"Okay."

"There is just one more little thing."

"What's that, Grandma?"

"Let's keep this party to ourselves, shall we?"

"Okay, but why?"

"We wouldn't want to upset Irene that we ate the last of her fudge sauce."

I had to laugh. I didn't know how Irene could possibly miss the fact the sauce was gone. Most of all, I couldn't imagine Irene upset about anything.

"Cross my heart," I said. "I'll never tell a soul."

Thirty

Mr. Martin stood next to me and surveyed the load of lumber in Mr. Spencer's truck. I was sure he thought my plan was crazy, but I had to ask.

"What do you think, Mr. Martin?"

His old felt hat was pushed back from his face. Several strands of grey hair poked out from under the hatband. He looked older and more exhausted than when we cleaned out the storeroom.

"Got enough wood?"

"This should be the last load," I said.

"An' I don't have ta pound nails?"

I smiled at him. He was a grumpy old man, but his quirkiness was growing on me.

"That's right, Mr. Martin," I said. "Jim's crew will do all the heavy work."

He pulled a crumpled handkerchief from his pocket and wiped at his runny nose. I didn't know if he carried the same hankie every day. I just knew it was always greyish white and always crumpled.

"I'm goin' in ta' have me a cup," he said, shoving the handkerchief back inside his pocket. "Holler if ya need me."

After he left, I inspected the wood. A lot of it was weathered, but some of the boards were in pristine condition. Jim wouldn't tell me where he found any of it.

"How do you suppose somebody comes up with this much lumber?" I said to myself.

The lumber already stacked along the building looked like enough to build the steps and fence. With the new load added to that, it looked like enough for an entire house.

"Good morning, Shirley."

Jim's father stepped around the front of the building with a mug in his hand. He walked toward me along the edge of the patio instead of on the newly laid limestone.

"Good morning, Mr. Spencer."

"Looks like the mason did a good job."

"He did a wonderful job," I said.

We stood without speaking for several minutes, admiring the work. All the while, Mr. Spencer whistled a cheery tune I didn't recognize.

When he stopped whistling, he looked me square in the eye. He wore a smile as wide and toothy as his son's.

"It's a beautiful day isn't it, Shirley?"

"Yes, it is," I said. "Why are you smiling at me like that?"

"Because you've made my son very happy."

"I'm just living up to my end of our agreement."

He gave me a quick pat on the back and pulled off his hat. He wiped sweat from his forehead with his sleeve.

"There for a while he forgot who his real friends are," he said. "Betty was no good for him."

"I didn't have anything to do with him breaking up with her."

"I know."

"I just agreed to let him spend time with George for helping with Grandma's patio."

"Thank you for that," he said. "It means the world to him."

Without another word, Mr. Spencer put on his hat and walked back to the cafe. All the while, he whistled the same tune I didn't know.

As he disappeared around the front of the building, I heard the rumble of engines behind me. When I turned around, two trucks pulled up along the back edge of the lot. The beds of both trucks were filled with boys of all ages.

Before the engines stopped, all of them jumped over the sides and tailgates. They ran so fast across the lot, I was afraid they would trample me, but they didn't. They stopped about three feet away.

They were dressed in faded jeans and T-shirts and looked eager to work. One of the youngest boys stepped forward and spoke for all of them.

"Hey, boss lady," he said. "Where do you want us to start?"

I fought hard to keep from laughing. I'd never been called boss before, and I definitely wasn't the boss on that job.

Before I could explain it to them, Jim came around the back of the building. He held George under his arm like a football, and stopped beside me.

"Good morning, boys," he said. "Welcome to Mrs. Ivey's patio."

There was murmuring all around and a lot of head shaking. A couple of the older boys even laughed.

"Crew," he said. "This is Shirley, the designer of the project."

Oh, dear. In one sentence, Jim put any blame with the design squarely on my shoulders.

"Thank you for coming to help," I said.

There was more murmuring and more head shaking. I decided they weren't used to working for a girl. Thank goodness Jim was the real person in charge.

"Grandma says you're welcome to go inside anytime for food and drinks," I said. "That is, whenever the foreman gives you a break."

I felt silly calling Jim the foreman, and I smiled at him. When he didn't smile back, I realized how serious he was about the job. I wiped the smile off my face.

"Here, Shirley, take George," he said. "Don't let him walk on the lot again until I tell you he can."

"Why can't he walk on the lot?"

Jim let out a loud sigh. I could see he was losing patience with me.

"There'll be loose nails everywhere," he said. "We don't want anything bad to happen to him."

"No, we don't," I said. "Never again."

I think Jim heard what I said. He just chose to ignore me in front of the boys.

I took George from him and cradled the little pug in my arms. He wagged his tail, and his whole body moved.

"Come on, George," I said. "Let's get some breakfast and let these boys do their work."

On the way to the front door, I had to wind around spectators lined up along the sidewalk. Grandma's patio was all the talk, and watching the construction was a big event for Willowdale.

Thirty-one

Marie stood at the café's front window and stared across the street. Personally, she didn't want to think about Elaine Carter and the coffee shop. Her business sense told her she had no choice.

"Ye gods and little fishes," she said. "Have you seen what that woman is doing now?"

Irene hurried from the kitchen, wiping her hands on the front of her apron. The braid down her back wagged back and forth as she walked.

"What's she doin'?"

"Last week, her sign read if you bought one muffin, the second muffin was half price."

"Yeah, I saw that one."

"This week, she's offering a free cup of coffee with the purchase of a cinnamon roll."

Her cook stood beside her at the window and let out a loud huff. She swung her braid around to the front of her and twisted the end of it in her fingers.

"What's she doin' next week?" she said. "Givin' away the store if you buy a piece of coffee cake?"

"That would be funny, Irene, if the situation weren't so serious."

Marie sat down on the chair next to Robert's with the green cushion. She scanned the columns on the ledger in front of her and shook her head. Her profits suffered when bus passengers ate pastries at the coffee shop instead of a meal at the café.

In addition to that, she agreed to provide free food to the volunteers building the fence. After a week of construction, the strain on the café's budget was beginning to show.

"I had forgotten how much food boys consume."

"That's okay," Irene said. "I don't mind doin' all that cookin'."

She missed the point entirely, but that was alright. Marie wasn't about to discuss her money concerns with her cook.

"You have worked very hard through all of this, Irene," she said. "I can't thank you enough."

"No need to thank me," Irene said. "That's what friends are for."

Marie glanced across the dining room at the new French doors in the side wall. There was a curtain hung on the outside of them. Jim didn't want her or her customers to see the construction before it was finished.

"You must be wonderin' what they're doin' out there."

"We shouldn't have to wait much longer to find out, Irene," she said. "At least I hope not."

Irene walked back to the kitchen, and Marie sat up a little straighter. She closed the café's ledger and pushed it away from her. She was tired of constantly worrying about money.

"This might be my last summer in Willowdale," she said to herself. "I'm not about to spoil my granddaughter's fun."

Irene shouted from the kitchen, "Everybody'll love the patio, Marie."

She hoped Irene was right, but there was no guarantee. She was competing against Elaine Carter, a very savvy business woman.

Marie picked up the ledger, walked behind the lunch counter and locked it inside the safe. She was determined to put business out of her mind if only for a little while.

She reached for the bucket of dirty table rags to carry them to the kitchen. Before she even touched the handle, Jimmy burst through the back door. He ran through the dining room and up to the counter.

"Mrs. Ivey," he said. "You need to come with me."

He was out of breath, and he shifted his weight from one foot to the other. She had never seen him so agitated.

"What is it Jimmy?" she said. "Is something wrong?"

"Hurry, Mrs. Ivey."

Without another word, he turned around and rushed back outside. Marie's imagination went wild, and she worried something happened to Shirley.

"What do you suppose is wrong, Irene?"

Before her cook could answer, she hurried to the rear of the café. She untied her apron, threw it on the floor and rushed out the back door.

Jimmy was standing at the corner of the building, waiting for her. He was still out of breath.

"What is it, Jimmy?"

"This way," he said, pointing toward the side of the building.

She followed him around the corner, but she didn't see an emergency. There were no workers in sight, and there were no sounds of construction.

"I don't see anything wrong, young man."

"On the patio, Mrs. Ivey," he said. "Hurry."

"Alright, alright," she said. "Could you walk a little slower?"

"There's no time to waste."

He swung open the hidden gate in the section of fence facing the alley. She tried to catch up to him, but he was too fast. He went into the patio and out of her sight before she could get there.

"Should I have brought first-aid supplies?"

She didn't wait for an answer and stepped through the gate. She stopped just inside.

The patio was crowded with the volunteer workers. All of them were clapping and cheering at her.

"Ye gods, Jimmy," she said, slapping both hands to her chest. "Are you trying to give me a heart attack?"

"Sorry, Mrs. Ivey," he said. "I didn't know how else to get you out here."

"Well done," she said. "I'm here."

Shirley stood in front of everyone, holding George in her arms. Her smile was as wide as Marie had ever seen it.

"Well, Grandma," she said. "What do you think?"

It grew very quiet, and Marie looked all around at the patio. She could feel the eyes of all the young people watching her.

"The fence and the steps are absolutely beautiful," she said to them. "Thank you for all your hard work."

While she tried to think of something else to say, Irene stepped through the gate. She held a tray of glasses filled with lemonade.

"I figured we could christen the patio with a little somethin' to drink."

"Did you know about this, Irene?"

"Of course," she said. "Have some lemonade."

After Marie took a glass, everyone else stepped up to get one. Jimmy stood on the first step leading to the French doors with his glass raised.

"A toast to Mrs. Ivey and her new patio," he said.

"A toast to all you boys for your hard work," Shirley said.

"Here, here," Marie said and took a sip from her glass.

Her granddaughter stood next to her with George sitting at her feet. She held her glass with two quivering hands, and Marie couldn't blame her for being nervous. The patio was her idea and her responsibility.

"Everything is beautiful, dear," she said. "I'm very proud of you."

"Thanks, Grandma."

Jimmy tapped the buckle on his watch band against his glass. Everyone stopped talking and turned toward him.

"We have one more thing to do, Mrs. Ivey."

"Oh, my," she said. "What more could there possibly be?"

He walked over to her and handed their glasses to Irene. He put his hand around her elbow and led her through the crowd. Together they walked up the steps to the curtain hiding the French doors.

"It's time to officially open your patio," he said.

There was more clapping and more cheering. Marie didn't know if she could stand any more excitement.

"I'll take hold of this side of the curtain, and you take hold of that side," he said.

"Then what, young man?"

"When I count to three, we pull down at the same time."

"Oh, my."

"Are you ready?"

"I believe so."

Marie looked over her shoulder, hoping to see Shirley. All she saw were the boys crowded around the foot of the steps. She wanted to wait and include her granddaughter in the ceremony, but Jimmy didn't give her the chance.

"Here we go," he said. "One, two, three—pull!"

Thirty-two

"Did you hear that, Aunt Elaine?"

Her aunt stopped plumping the pillows on one of the sofas and looked up at her. She didn't seem interested in what she had to say, so Betty tried a different approach.

"I think something might be wrong across the street."

That caught her attention. Her aunt walked over and stood beside her at the front window.

"I don't hear a sound, Betty," she said. "Must you continue to stand here and stare at that unsightly fence?"

Before Betty could describe what she heard, the noise came again. This time, it was louder.

"See, Aunt Elaine," she said. "I told you I heard something."

Her aunt went to the front door and pulled it open. She stood in the doorway with her arms folded across her chest.

"It seems Mrs. Ivey is hosting a party," she said.

Betty hurried over to the door and stood beside her aunt. The fence was too tall for her to see the activity on Mrs. Ivey's new patio.

"You taught me it isn't proper for a business to exclude another business from its celebrations."

"Of course, it isn't proper," her aunt said. "You must remember we're discussing Willowdale, after all."

"What do you mean?"

"Most of these people have lived here their entire lives and are not very sophisticated," she said. "I doubt they are even aware of proper business etiquette."

"I suppose."

Betty listened to the commotion at Ivey's Café for only another minute or two. She couldn't stand being excluded from the fun. She turned away from the door and plopped down on the nearest chair.

"I bet it was Shirley's idea not to invite us," she said. "She never did like me."

Her aunt ignored her, closed the door and began plumping the pillows on the other sofa. When her back was turned, Betty peeked out the window. What she saw infuriated her, and she jumped to her feet.

A rowdy group of boys poured out of the café's front door. Behind them were Shirley and Jim walking side by side. George was on his leash, pulling Shirley up the street.

"It must be time for that ugly little dog to use his fire hydrant," she said. "Why does Jim have to go along?"

Her aunt looked out the window, then at her. Even before she spoke, Betty knew what she was going to say.

"I have explained all of this to you over and over again."

"I know, Aunt Elaine," she said. "You don't think Jim is good enough for me."

"That's correct," she said. "You should be thankful he is no longer your concern."

Betty hurried to the nearest bookcase and picked up the dust rag she left there. She fought back her tears and pretended to dust a row of books.

"Thankful?" she whispered so her aunt couldn't hear. "Nobody steals a boy away from me."

While she flapped the dust rag above the books, her aunt walked over to her. She held a book in one hand and the coffee shop's mailbox key in the other.

"When you are finished dusting, put this book back in its proper location," she said. "After that, go to the bank and collect our mail."

"Yes, Aunt Elaine."

She took the book and dropped the key into her dress pocket. When her aunt walked into the gift shop, she laid the book and the rag on the shelf. She tiptoed to the front of the store, eased the door open and sneaked outside.

The only other people on the street were Jim and Shirley at the end of the block. The strange looking dog was pacing in front of the hydrant.

"If you think Jim is yours, Shirley," she whispered, "you'd better think again."

The two of them stood next to the hydrant, watching George sniff every blade of grass. They talked nonstop, but Betty was too far away to hear what they said.

They were so preoccupied with their conversation, Betty walked up the street unnoticed. At the bank, she opened the lobby door, slipped inside and closed the door behind her.

The bank was closed for the rest of the day, and the main door to get inside was locked. Without customers walking in or out, the mailbox area was the perfect place to hide.

"Let's just see what you two are doing," she said.

Hiding behind the glass door's wooden frame, she watched them talk. They didn't stop until the dog finished his business.

When he pulled against his leash, he nearly knocked Shirley down. Jim took the leash from her, and the odd little dog led them back to the café.

"The mail will just have to wait, Aunt Elaine," she said to herself. "I'm not going anywhere yet."

After a minute or two, Jim walked out of the cafe and climbed into his father's truck. He drove past the bank and turned onto the gravel road toward the mill.

Shortly after that, Shirley and her grandmother drove up the alley in the old truck. They turned onto 1st Street and stopped at the intersection. The old dog was sitting between them.

Betty ducked behind the door frame again and stayed hidden. When she looked outside again, the old truck was on Main Street moving in the direction of the county road.

"Finally, you're going home," she said.

She opened the lobby door, stepped outside and looked up and down Main Street. The stores were closed, and there weren't any other vehicles in sight.

"Here's my chance."

To avoid attracting her aunt's attention, she crossed the street and walked through the empty lot. At the fence, she peeked through a narrow space between two of the white-washed boards.

"I can't see a thing," she said.

She walked along the perimeter of the building and up the steps to the back door. She jiggling the handle, but the door was locked.

"That's too bad," she said. "I wonder—"

She walked back across the lot, along the sidewalk and up to the front door. She looked around to make sure no one saw her and opened the screen door. It only took one push on the main door lock, and the door swung open.

"My, my, Mrs. Ivey," she said. "How careless of you to leave the door unlocked."

After one last look up and down the street, she went inside and closed both doors. Everything in the front of the café was as she remembered except for the French doors in the side wall.

"Is anyone here?" she said.

There was no reply, so she went to the French doors and scanned the patio. It looked nicer than she expected.

"Not so bad," she said, "in a primitive sort of way."

Satisfied what she wanted wasn't out there, Betty walked straight to the back of the café. She was only a few steps inside the game room when she stopped.

"There they are," she said.

The pug's bed and bowls were in a corner of the room next to a potbellied stove. Although they were within direct sight of the dining room, they were also within easy reach of the back door.

"Perfect," she said.

Thirty-three

"I think we did a pretty good job," I said. "Don't you, Grandma?"

It was chilly so early in the morning, but I didn't mind. Grandma and I wanted to try out the new patio before the café opened for the day.

"It is the most beautiful patio I have ever seen," she said.

"Jim wouldn't tell me where he got all the building supplies."

"Oh?"

"He wouldn't even tell me what everything cost."

"Is that so?"

Grandma didn't seem interested in the details of the project, but I was determined. I wanted to know how he found all the materials and paid for them.

"Do you know, Grandma?"

She didn't answer my question. Instead, she put her feet on the chair across from her and sipped her coffee. It was obvious I wasn't going to get the facts from her.

I sat cross-legged on my chair with my hands wrapped around my cup. While I drank my hot chocolate, I looked around the patio.

The wooden fence the boys built was whitewashed and tinted with a hint of grey. Jim picked the perfect color to give the patio a touch of sophistication Grandma liked.

The tables and chairs they built were painted in a variety of muted colors, and the limestone pavers were rough under foot. Everything gave the patio a casual, lived-in feel the way Grandpa would have liked.

Jim managed to capture the perfect blend of their personalities. I mentally gave him another point in his favor.

"I don't know what I would have done without Jim's help," I said. "He knew exactly what to do and how to get it done."

"Yes, dear," Grandma said. "He has been a very good friend."

We sat quietly for several minutes, nursed our drinks and listened to two mourning doves. They were perched in one the saplings outside the fence, cooing to each other.

I decided the new patio was my second favorite place in the world to sit. My most favorite place was the tree swing at the farmhouse.

"I've been thinking," Grandma said.

"About what?"

"I don't think we should open the French doors to my customers this morning."

"Why not, Grandma?" I said. "Everything's ready."

"I believe we should wait and host a grand opening party."

"A party?"

"It would be a glorious way to introduce this beautiful space to Willowdale, don't you think?"

I uncrossed my legs and put my feet down. George was asleep on his blanket under the table, and I was careful not to step on him.

"I love that idea," I said. "Let's do it."

"I'll call everyone right now and set up a meeting."

Thirty-four

"This won't take long," Miss Spitz said. "Would everyone sit down, please?"

She stood at the front of the church's meeting room, waving a sheet of paper in the air. No one paid any attention to her.

Almost everyone was in line at the refreshment table. They were waiting for their turn at the store-bought cookies and cupcakes Jim brought back from Monticello.

"Can't we do something to help her, Grandma?"

We were seated in the first row of chairs, and Grandma was supposed to be in charge. At that moment, it didn't feel like anyone was in charge of anything.

Mr. Martin walked past the line at the refreshment table and up to Miss Spitz. He drank the last of his coffee, took the paper from her and handed her his empty cup.

"Put that on the table fer me," he said.

"What in the world?"

"Go on," he said. "I'll git 'em ta sit down."

Miss Spitz huffed at him. She set his cup on the refreshment table and walked to the first row of chairs. She huffed one more time and sat on the chair next to me.

"Of all things," she said.

Mr. Martin pushed his way through the refreshment line, ignoring all the complaints. He stopped in front of the percolator on the end of the table.

After he folded Miss Spitz's paper in half, he pulled a pen from his breast pocket. He scribbled something on the paper, but I couldn't see what it was.

"Line's closed," he shouted so everyone could hear.

He skewered his makeshift sign on the spout of the percolator and turned around. The next person in line was a muscular man at least a foot taller than he was.

For several seconds, they stood facing each other without saying a word. The man looked intimidating, but Mr. Martin stood his ground.

"That sign says there's no more coffee," the man said. "What's that supposed to mean?"

"Means no more coffee," Mr. Martin said. "Ya might as well sit down."

The people in line behind the muscular man grumbled and glared at Mr. Martin. I was afraid there might be a fight, but nobody challenged him.

"I'm coming back after the meeting," the man with the muscles said.

"Ya do that."

Mr. Martin stayed there until the last person moved away. When everyone was seated, he sat down at the other end of the first row.

Pastor Lawrence stood up and walked to the front of the room. He nodded at Mr. Martin.

"Thank you for your help."

"Yer welcome, Pastor."

"As for the rest of you," he said. "There will be ample time to eat and visit when the meeting is finished."

Miss Spitz scooted to the edge of her chair and raised her hand. It reminded me of a student at school trying to catch the teacher's attention.

"Yes, Harriet," the pastor said.

"Isn't Marie supposed to be in charge of the meeting?"

There was a lot of whispering behind us. I wanted Grandma to get up and say something. If she didn't, there would be no stopping the crowd from going back to the refreshment table.

"Yes, Harriet," Grandma finally said. "I was just about to speak."

When she stood up, Pastor Lawrence sat back down in the second row of chairs. Grandma walked forward and took his place at the front of the room.

Her cheeks were flushed, and her hands shook. A stray hair hung from the bun at the nape of her neck. She didn't bother to put it back in place, and that wasn't like her.

"We're here today because I need your help," she said.

"Not again," one of the men said.

"It isn't exactly the same as last time," Grandma said. "My granddaughter and I want to host a party at the café."

Before she could explain, people began peppering her with questions. I couldn't turn around fast enough to see who was asking.

"Yeah, so?"

"What's that got to do with any of us?"

"This isn't going to be another birthday party, is it?"

Grandma cleared her throat and looked at me. She pulled her handkerchief out from under her belt and mopped at perspiration on her forehead.

"No, it isn't going to be a birthday party," she said. "We want to celebrate the opening of my café's new patio."

I didn't know why she looked so uncomfortable, but I couldn't stand watching her suffer. I swallowed back my nerves, stood up and turned toward the crowd.

"That last storm left some of you with a lot of damage to fix," I said.

"We know that, missy," a bald man in the third row said.

I tried to ignore his rudeness. It wasn't easy.

"What I mean is," I said, "you haven't had time for your potluck."

"Potluck?" he said. "What are you talking about?"

Grandma walked up to me and put her hand on my shoulder. I wasn't explaining myself very well, and I was glad she took over.

"What my granddaughter means is," she said, "we would like to combine our patio's grand opening with Willowdale's annual potluck."

Grandma didn't need my help, and I was sure nobody wanted to listen to me talk. I sat down and sank low in my chair.

"That sounds like a wonderful idea," the pastor said.

There was head shaking and mumbling, and I heard snickering at the back of the room. We all turned toward the noise.

A high-school-aged couple, dressed all in black, sat alone in the back row. They slouched and propped their feet on the chairs in front of them. The girl snapped her chewing gum in a steady rhythm.

I couldn't imagine why Grandma invited them to her meeting, but she must have had a reason. She always did.

Pastor Lawrence stood up. He walked to the back of the room and faced the couple.

"You have something you want to say?" he said.

With everyone staring at them, the couple's cocky smiles faded. They dropped their feet to the floor and sat up straight. The girl stopped snapping her gum, but neither of them said a word.

"Nothing?" the pastor said. "Let's hear what Mrs. Ivey has to say."

We all turned back around, and Grandma stuffed the hankie back under her belt. The perspiration on her forehead was gone, and her voice was stronger.

"It will be a potluck as always," she said. "We will hold it at the café on the new patio and the rest of the lot."

"Like last summer?" Horace Wilson said.

"That's exactly what I have in mind," Grandma said. "Except it won't be on July fourth, and it won't be in the high school gym."

I had to laugh. There was only one thing both plans had in common. Both were potlucks.

"Mrs. Ivey?"

The rude boy in the back row raised his hand. The girl beside him sat quietly and stared at him with wide eyes.

"Yes, Kenny," Grandma said.

The boy stood up and straightened his black T-shirt over the waist of his pants. He looked familiar, but I couldn't quite place him until he spoke.

"My dance band played for you last year," he said. "You want us to play again?"

"Yes, indeed," she said. "That would be most generous of you and your band."

After that, the room came alive with suggestions and offers of help. It reminded me of my first summer working in Willowdale. The residents always pulled together in good times and bad.

"And they know how to throw really great potlucks," I said.

"Did you say something, dear?"

"I was just thinking out loud, that's all."

Thirty-five

There was a lot of work to do before the combined potluck and grand opening. I hardly knew where to begin.

The dining room needed scrubbing from top to bottom, and the furniture needed rearranging. Outside, I had to find a place for the dance band and the patio's tables and chairs.

"Where should we put all the food?" I said to myself. "Inside or outside?"

"Are you talking to yourself again?"

Jim pushed open the screen door. His arms were loaded with newspapers, and he let the door slam shut behind him.

"I guess I am," I said.

"Well, just ignore me," he said. "I'll put these by the rack and get out of your way."

His baseball cap was pushed back away from his face, and he wore an annoying smile. Did he enjoy sneaking up like that and embarrassing me?

"Don't worry," I said. "I never have a problem ignoring you."

That was a boldface lie. It couldn't have been further from the truth, but I wasn't about to let him know it.

Grandma came around the lunch counter, wiping her hands on her apron. Her attention was focused on something outside.

"Here's the bus," she said. "You make certain those papers and magazines are in proper order, young lady."

"Yes, Grandma."

When she used that tone, I knew it was time to get my mind off the potluck plans. They would have to wait until after the café closed for the day.

It was more important to keep the bus passengers happy. We wanted them to eat a meal at the café, not go over to the coffee shop.

"I've got some extra time," Jim said, tossing his cap on the nearest table. "Let me help."

I didn't argue with him. We removed the old newspapers and restacked the rack with the new ones. He carried the old papers to the back door, and I arranged the magazines in alphabetical order. That was my special touch, not something Grandma required.

Jim walked back to the front of the café, and I heard the back door open and close. I assumed it was Mr. Martin, and I grabbed the truck's key ring from under the counter.

It was Mr. Martin's job to load the papers in the truck. It was my job to haul all that paper to the dump.

"Wait a minute, Shirley," Jim said. "I don't think you want to leave yet."

"Why's that?"

"I think you have company."

"What?"

He was at the front window looking at the bus from Lafayette parked in front of the café. I looked outside, too, but I couldn't figure out what he was talking about. All I saw were strangers getting off the bus.

When the bus finally pulled away, passengers scattered in all directions. Some of them walked across the street to Miss Carter's coffee shop. The rest headed to Grandma's café.

Once the crowd thinned out even more, I saw what Jim meant. Grandma was at the curb with her arms around one of the passengers. There was no mistaking who it was.

"Aunt Maude!"

I put the key ring back under the counter and ran to the front door. I hadn't seen Aunt Maude since the night she got sick last summer.

Jim opened the door and held it for me. I pushed right past him and rushed outside without a thought to his feelings.

When Grandma stopped hugging Aunt Maude, I threw my arms around her neck. I was surprised how much weight she lost and how frail she looked after only a year.

"What a wonderful surprise," I said. "Have you come back for good?"

"Now, now, young lady," Grandma said. "There will be plenty of time to talk about all of that later."

Aunt Maude pushed me away and held me at arm's length for a moment. When Jim stepped forward, she let go of me and reached out her hand to him.

"I am so happy to see all of you," she said.

Jim dropped Aunt Maude's suitcase on the sidewalk and put his arms around her. She held him gently and rocked him back and forth.

Grandma told me he thought of Aunt Maude as a second mother after his own mother passed away. I could see she felt the same, and I regretted being so thoughtless at the door a minute ago.

I wiped at my tears with the back of my hand and went inside. There was a little pug asleep in the game room. He would want to see Aunt Maude right away.

Thirty-six

"You make the best scrambled eggs, Shirley."

"Thank you."

Aunt Maude scooped up another forkful of the eggs followed by a bite of toast. It was her third helping of breakfast, and I wondered why she was so thin. Didn't she get enough to eat at her brother's house?

"Can I have another piece of toast?"

"Of course," I said.

I got up and put more bread in the toaster while Grandma paced between the sink and the phone on the wall. I didn't know why she was pacing, but she always paced when she was upset.

"Are you alright, Grandma?"

"I'm fine."

Seeing her pace made me dizzy, and I stopped watching. I knew she would tell us what was bothering her when she was ready.

"Sit down, Marie, before you wear out the floor," Aunt Maude said.

Grandma walked over to the table and sat down. Without a word, she rested her arms on the table and folded her hands.

Aunt Maude finished the food on her plate, sat up straight and cleared her throat. She looked at Grandma.

"Marie," she said. "I'm grateful my brother took me in when I was so sick."

"Yes, William is a kind and generous man."

"I've tried to make Illinois my home, but I can't," she said. "Your invitation to come visit was just what I needed to cheer me up."

"What's the matter with Illinois?" I said.

Grandma gave me one of her stern looks, and I knew what that meant. I had spoken out of turn.

"It isn't about Illinois," Aunt Maude said.

She pushed her plate away. Instead of her usual pleasant smile, she looked somber.

"I love my brother, but Willowdale is my home," she said. "When I left here it was like leaving my family behind."

"Willowdale isn't the same without you," I said, "and George really missed you, too."

I sat down, leaned over and peeked under the table to check on the little pug. His eyes were wide open, and he looked right at me. His tail wagged, but he didn't lift his chin off Aunt Maude's shoe.

When I sat back up, Grandma reached across the table and gave her hand a pat. I wondered how life could be so cruel as to tear two best friends apart.

"Maude," she said. "It's time for me to retire from the café business."

My mouth dropped open. She had told me about her money troubles, but she never talked about retirement. I couldn't begin to imagine it.

"What do you mean, Grandma?"

She scooted her chair away from the table and leaned against the backrest. She looked straight at me.

"Young people don't understand how quickly life passes," she said.

I couldn't argue with that. I was still too young to really know about the passage of time.

"One moment, you're a new bride," she said. "The next moment, you're a widow managing a home and a café."

She looked away from me and over at Aunt Maude. She smiled and sat up straighter in her chair.

"That is why I think both of you will approve of what I have done."

Before she could explain, the toast popped up. I jumped up, grabbed it out of the toaster and sat back down. I laid the toast on Aunt Maude's plate and pushed the butter dish closer to her.

"What is it, Grandma?" I said. "What did you do?"

She pulled her chair back up to the table. It seemed like forever before she spoke.

"Shirley, dear," she said. "Do you remember when I spoke to you about my financial difficulties?"

"I remember, Grandma."

"Since our conversation," she said, "I have continued to struggle to pay the loans on the house and the café."

"When you never said anything more about it, I thought things were better."

"I didn't want to worry you."

Not worry me? How could I not worry? Grandpa and my great grandparents left all their financial problems for her to deal with alone.

"The café is doing better with the game room," I said. "It should do even better with the new patio."

"I'm sure it will."

"I don't understand."

"I simply owe too much money."

I wanted desperately to make things better for her. I blurted out the first thing that came to mind.

"Remember the man from the bus?" I said. "He thought you should rent out the game room once in a while."

Grandma leaned back in her chair and shook her head. Her grey hair hung freely around her shoulders and made her look years older.

"If I were younger, that might be a viable option," she said. "Running the café at my age has become too physically exhausting."

"I never knew you felt that way, Grandma."

"Well, I do, and I talked with Gene Daily at the bank about it," she said. "He was a big help to me."

"Help with what?"

"I decided to sell the café and this house," she said, "and he found a buyer for them."

She was really going to sell the café and the house. I was pretty sure my mouth dropped open again. I knew I couldn't breathe.

"What do you think, dear?"

She stared at me, and I struggled to think of the right words to say. When I finally caught my breath, I could only think of one thing.

"Do you know who the buyer is?"

"Yes, I do, and it is extremely complicated."

Oh, dear. It wasn't enough my whole world was falling down around me. I had to deal with complications, too.

"The sale isn't completed," she said. "When everyone in town learns the details, however, they will most certainly think I've lost my mind."

"That's not possible," Aunt Maude said. "You're the most sensible person I know."

"I used to think so myself."

"What makes it so complicated, Grandma?"

"I'd like to know, too, Marie."

The wall phone rang before Grandma could say more, and I ran to answer it. Who would call Grandma so early in the morning?

"Hello, Miss Spitz," I said into the receiver.

"Good morning, Shirley," the operator said. "Gene Daily is on the line for your grandmother."

"It's Mr. Daily, Grandma."

I held my hand over the receiver and waited for her to walk across the kitchen. When she took the phone from me, I sat back down at the table.

"Hello, Gene," she said. "Yes, of course. We will be there before I open the café."

She hung up the receiver and turned around. Her hands were trembling.

"Gene has the preliminary paperwork ready," she said. "He just needs our signatures, Maude."

"Why in the world would he need my signature?"

Aunt Maude and I looked at each other. She seemed as confused as I felt, and I shrugged my shoulders.

I didn't know what Grandma was up to. Whatever it was, she needed more than one signature.

Thirty-seven

Mr. Martin sat down on a patio chair and took a deep breath. The town was about to descend on the café, and he wasn't sure he was up for it.

"I'm gittin' too old fer all this."

"You're not that old, Mr. Martin," Shirley said.

She stood at the bottom of the steps, surveying the patio. Her arms were loaded with napkins and paper plates.

He looked around at the folding tables Mrs. Ivey borrowed from the church. The four of them and one little table in the corner filled the entire patio area.

"Ya got enough tables?"

"I think so," she said. "There should be just enough room for all the potluck dishes."

"Yer really gonna put the food outside?"

"That way everything's handy," she said. "They can either eat inside the café or outside the fence on the patio tables."

He didn't understand why anybody would put food tables outside. He had had enough of that in the Army, but that was Shirley's responsibility, not his.

He looked out the wide-open gate in the fence. Cars and trucks were parked along the alley, and people walked across the lot. Everybody carried a dish in their hands.

"I best git goin'," he said. "Yer grandma wants me ta greet all these folks."

"Before you go," Shirley said. "What do you think of the banner the Sunday school class made?"

Mr. Martin stood up and studied the sign strung along the inside of the fence. It was made of white butcher paper and was lashed to the fence with baling twine. "WELCOME TO OUR NEW PATIO" was printed in red crayon along its full length.

"It's okay," he said.

On the other side of the fence, Kenny's dance band was playing "The Purple People Eater". It was loud and off beat, and it made his head hurt.

"When're those boys gonna take a break?" he said. "Give these ol' ears a rest."

"It won't be for quite a while," Shirley said. "Everybody loves their music."

He grumbled and put on his old felt hat. Shirley moved out of his way, and he walked up the steps to the French doors. The dining room was packed, and he had to elbow his way through the crowd to get inside.

Before he got halfway across the room, Harriet Spitz walked up to him. She jammed her fists on her hips.

"Aren't you supposed to be standing at the front door, Mr. Martin?"

He gave her a nod of his head and pushed past her. He didn't need a busybody like Harriet telling him where he was supposed to be.

When he got to the front door, he practically ran into Elaine Carter and her niece. They were all dressed up in fancy city clothes, and Betty carried a small tray. It was covered with crackers topped with cheese and meat and things he couldn't identify.

"Well, now," he said. "What da ya call those?"

"Those, Mr. Martin, are canapes," Miss Carter said. "Perhaps you'll try one later."

"Maybe."

"If you'll excuse me," she said. "I want to find Marie and congratulate her on the new patio."

He was surprised Miss Carter stopped to speak to him, but her niece didn't even say hello. She walked right by him and headed in the direction of the patio with the tray. He lost sight of her when she melded into the crowd.

That was alright with him. He had a job to do. He didn't have time to think about Miss Carter or her niece.

He hung his hat on a hook beside the magazine rack and went to work greeting guests. He knew most of the adults, but none of the children looked familiar.

"Where'd all these young'uns come from?"

The minute they arrived, they broke free of their parents. With their voices on full volume, they chased each other around the dining room unsupervised.

Just when he thought he couldn't tolerate another screaming child, he felt a hand on his arm. It was Mrs. Ivey dressed in her navy-blue dress with the white lace collar.

"Go get something to eat, Mr. Martin," she said.

He barely heard her over the din, but he didn't want to leave his post. Watching the front door was the only job he had.

"I'll git me somethin' later."

"That just won't do," she said. "You get something to eat right now, and I'll stand here until you get back."

"Yes, ma'am."

He knew it wouldn't do any good to argue with her. He left her standing by the front door and edged his way through the crowd.

There was a steady stream of people going up and down the steps with platefuls of food. He had to wait his turn to get to the patio.

When he finally got to the bottom of the steps, Shirley stood behind one of the tables. She was scolding a youngster for taking too many of Aunt Maude's chocolate chip cookies.

The little boy rushed past him and ran up the steps. At the top step he stopped, turned around and stuck his tongue out at her.

"I'm telling my mommy on you," he said and ran into the dining room.

Mr. Martin walked over to Shirley and laughed. He'd forgotten how childish children could be.

"Don't ya worry none," he said. "His mama won't hear him in all the noise."

"Thank you, Mr. Martin," she said. "That makes me feel a little better."

He grabbed a paper plate and walked up and down the four folding tables. Even though more food was arriving, most of his favorite dishes were picked clean.

"Guess I'm stuck with beans," he said.

Shirley followed behind him and picked up empty serving dishes. She added them to the pile of dirty dishes on the small table in the corner.

"At least I rescued a few of Aunt Maude's cookies," she said.

While Mr. Martin scraped the last helping of baked beans onto his plate, Jimmy ran through the gate. He was out of breath, and his shoes were covered in dust.

"Mr. Martin," he said. "Have you seen George?"

"What do you mean?" Shirley said. "He's asleep in the game room."

"I just checked," he said. "He isn't there."

"Did you check behind the lunch counter and in the kitchen?"

"Of course, I checked there."

"Well, he isn't out here," she said. "I've been here most of the time."

Mr. Martin didn't much care for the little dog, but George meant everything to Aunt Maude. If anything happened to him, he didn't know what she would do.

Just the thought took his appetite away. He set his plate of uneaten beans on the corner of the nearest folding table.

"Maybe ya oughta check with Betty," he said.

"Why would we want to do that?" Shirley said.

"I'm thinkin' she has an ax ta grind with both of ya."

Shirley didn't hesitate another second. She spun around, ran up the steps and disappeared into the crowd.

Jimmy rushed out the fence gate, dodging little children in his way. Mr. Martin watched him circle the lot. He talked to everyone at the tables and all the boys in the dance band.

Mr. Martin knew Mrs. Ivey was waiting for him at the front door. She was probably tired of all the commotion and wondered what was keeping him.

"Hate ta do it," he said, "but I gotta stay here."

George was missing. He figured helping Jimmy and Shirley find him was more important than greeting his neighbors.

He sat down on a patio chair and waited. When they came back a few minutes later, there was fear written all over their faces.

"I didn't see George or Betty anywhere inside," Shirley said.

"They aren't outside, either," Jimmy said. "Nobody out there has seen either one of them."

Mr. Martin stood up. His paper plate was still on the corner of the table, but he wasn't hungry. He grabbed it and tossed the whole thing into the garbage barrel beside the steps.

"Go git yer grandpa's truck keys, Shirley," he said.

She didn't say a word or ask any questions. She ran up the steps and into the dining room.

He stood with Jimmy beside the gate and waited for her. They didn't have to wait long.

Shirley stepped through the French doors, stood on the top step and looked down at them. There were tears in her eyes.

"What's wrong, Shirley?" Jimmy said.

"The truck keys are gone."

"Maybe your grandma moved them."

"I don't think so," she said.

"Why not?"

"I left Grandpa's truck parked by the back door, and it isn't there anymore."

Thirty-eight

Jim pulled his father's truck to the back door of the café. I climbed inside with George's blanket in my hand. I folded it and laid it on the seat between us.

"Did your grandma see you leave?"

"No," I said. "I decided she and Aunt Maude would find out about George soon enough."

"Good idea."

"Maybe he just wandered off again," I said.

"He wouldn't do that with Aunt Maude here."

I was sick with worry, but I forced myself not to cry. Little George needed us to stay strong.

"Jim," I said. "Do you think Betty would hurt him?"

"I don't know."

He didn't say any more about it, and that was fine with me. Both of us were worried. Nothing more needed to be said.

Jim drove west out of town. We were almost to Cemetery Road when he pulled the truck onto the shoulder and stopped.

"What's the matter?" I said.

"We can't just drive around," he said. "We'll never find them that way."

For a minute or two, we sat without speaking while the truck's engine idled. I didn't know enough about the area to know where to begin looking for them. I just hoped George was safe.

"He's never been anywhere with Betty before," I said.

"They're in your grandpa's truck, and he's used to that."

I rested my hand on George's blanket. It was covered with his fawn hair, and I laughed.

"What's so funny?"

"They say pugs don't shed very much, but just look how much George sheds," I said.

Jim laughed with me, but our laughter didn't last long. The thought of George being at Betty's mercy sent a chill through me.

"I wonder—" Jim said.

"What?"

"There's a place she really liked when we were out picking wildflowers."

I twisted in the seat and looked at him. His jaw was tight, and the knuckles on his hands were white from strangling the steering wheel.

"What're we waiting for?" I said. "Let's go."

Jim pulled the truck back onto the road and turned at Cemetery Road. He drove so fast on the pothole-riddled gravel, the truck kicked up a cloud of dust. I rolled up my window to keep it out of the cab.

I recognized some of the roads from last summer, but Jim turned too many times. It wasn't long before I was completely disoriented.

"Are we almost there?"

Without warning, Jim slammed his foot on the brake. I pressed my hands against the dashboard and braced myself against hitting the windshield. The truck skidded to a stop.

"We're here," he said.

We were stopped in front of a two-story farmhouse covered in peeling white paint. Grandpa's truck was nowhere in sight, and the place appeared to be abandoned. The only signs of life were chickens pecking at the ground and a collie running toward us.

"Where are we?" I said.

"This is Horace Wilson's place, and that dog is Sebastian."

"What do we do now?"

"We stay in the truck."

Jim leaned out his window and called to the dog, but the collie didn't slow down. He hit the driver's door with both front feet and stood on his back legs. He bared his teeth and growled at us.

"You remember me, Sebastian," Jim said. "We're just going to drive on through, okay?"

The dog shifted his gaze from Jim to me. He eyed me as though I were a fresh piece of meat.

"Hi, Sebastian."

"That's Shirley," Jim said. "She's okay."

The dog stopped growling, dropped to the ground and backed up a few feet. After a couple of seconds, he ran back to his lookout on the front porch. He curled up on an old rug and rested his chin on his front feet.

"Wow," I said and waited for my heart to quit pounding.

"Now he knows who you are, and he won't bother you again."

"Okay," I said. "If you say so."

Jim shifted the truck into first gear and pulled into the driveway. He eased forward across the barnyard and around several dilapidated outbuildings. Behind the last one was a dirt track just wide enough for the truck.

"What now?" I said.

"We follow this track to a place I wanted to show you," he said. "It just wasn't supposed to be today or like this."

Along one side of the track was a fence separating the corn fields on both sides of us. Along the other side of the truck was a small creek nearly hidden by tall weeds and wild rose bushes. Jim inched forward and maneuvered his truck between the fence and the creek.

The narrow track dead-ended at a stand of birch trees. Grandpa's truck was parked in front of them, and Jim pulled to a stop next to it. He turned off the engine, grabbed the keys and got out of the truck.

"We walk from here," he said. "We'll deal with your truck later."

I jumped out of the cab and looked through the driver's window of Grandpa's truck. The keys were in the ignition, but George wasn't there.

"Let's go, Shirley."

I followed him along a winding, well-worn footpath. It led us deep into the woods where the air reeked of rotting leaves. The smell reminded me more of autumn than summer.

After several minutes, the woods and the footpath ended at the edge of a narrow sandy beach. Beyond the beach was an enormous pond surrounded on three sides by hardwood trees.

At the upper end of the pond, the small creek we followed flowed into it. At the lower end was an earthen dam.

Betty was standing on the dam with her back to us. She wore the same cotton dress and white patent leather shoes she wore to the party.

I wanted to shout at her and ask about George, but I didn't want to make matters worse. I kept quiet and followed Jim along the edge of the sand. When we got to the dam, we stopped within a few feet of her.

"Hi, Betty," he said in a quiet, measured tone. "What're you doing?"

"I'm looking at your pond and all the pretty trees."

She turned around, and I forced myself not to react. She held George in her arms and tears streamed down her cheeks.

"You brought her?" she said when she saw me.

"We were worried about you," Jim said.

"Is that right, Shirley?" she said. "You were worried about me?"

I was known for my honesty, and I wasn't going to lie to her. George's safety was at stake.

"No, not really," I said. "I wanted to find George."

"Shirley!" Jim said. "What're you doing?"

"It's okay, Jim," Betty said. "Shirley and I will never be friends."

She stepped back a couple of feet further away from me. The move took her closer to the edge of the dam.

When George saw Jim and me, his tail wagged. His whole body wiggled, and Betty struggled to hang on to him.

I wanted to run and grab the little pug, but I was afraid of what she would do. I needed to be patient and wait for the right moment.

"Why did you come here, Betty?" Jim said.

"I wanted to visit our special place again."

"You're missing the grand opening potluck."

"I don't care."

"When your aunt can't find you," he said, "she'll be worried sick."

"She won't miss me."

"Why would you say that?"

"All she cares about is her stupid coffee shop."

The longer she talked to Jim, the more desperate she sounded. I actually felt sorry for her.

"Why did you bring George?" he said.

"I wanted to see you."

"I don't understand," Jim said. "We're not dating anymore."

"That's why I brought him," she said. "I wasn't sure you'd come looking for me, but I knew you'd come looking for this dog."

Jim took one step forward. As he did, Betty took another step backwards—right to the edge of the dam. He reached out to grab her arm to stop her.

Betty freed one hand from around George and tried to bat his hand away. She missed his hand and hit his chest.

The force of the blow knocked Jim backwards. He flailed his arms and tried to regain his footing on the uneven surface.

It didn't work, and there was nothing to stop his momentum. He fell off the back of the dam and tumbled all the way down the rocky spillway. He landed facedown at the bottom of the cut, motionless.

"Jim!"

I listened for an answer. There wasn't one.

I was furious with Betty, and I wanted to scream at her. I didn't get the chance.

The blow threw her off balance. Her dress shoes slipped on the packed soil, and George's added weight made her top heavy. She squeezed the pug tighter as she toppled backwards into the pond.

"George!"

I wanted to climb down to Jim and make sure he was okay, but I didn't have time. My immediate concern was for Betty and George.

I ran to the spot where they fell in and looked over the edge. George was close to the dam, paddling as fast as his short legs could move.

With his unwebbed feet and bulky body, he wasn't making any headway. He was sinking, and the only thing above water was the tip of his nose.

"Hang on, big guy."

I dropped to my stomach and reached my arm out as far as I could. Before he slipped completely below the surface, I managed to hook my fingers around his collar. I pulled him toward me with all my strength.

When he was close enough, I reached with my other hand and grabbed the scruff of his neck. I pulled him the rest of the way with both hands and dragged him onto the dam.

He rolled onto his stomach and coughed a couple of times. When he stood up and shook the water off his back, I knew he was okay.

"You stay right there, George."

I jumped to my feet and scanned the surface of the pond. I looked for any sign of Betty. There was nothing. She simply disappeared.

"Where are you?"

After a second or two, I saw bubbles rise to the surface about fifteen feet away. There were so many of them, I knew she was in trouble.

Instinctively, I yanked off my shoes and socks and jumped into the water. I swam toward the bubbles and did one surface dive after another, searching for her.

The water was murky, and the visibility was nearly zero. I swung my arms back and forth in front of me, relying on my sense of touch.

After several dives, I stopped to catch my breath. I almost lost hope of finding her until I saw two more bubbles.

I did a surface dive right above them and swam toward the bottom of the pond. My ear drums ached from the pressure, but I kept going down. I never stopped swinging my arms back and forth.

I was running out of air, and my lungs burned. I couldn't stay down much longer.

I swung my arms one last time and felt her hair. I grabbed a fistful of it and swam toward the surface. Her soaked cotton dress tried to drag us down. I kicked as hard as I could.

I finally burst through the pond's surface and gulped a lungful of air. I kept kicking my feet and pulling on Betty's hair.

When she bobbed to the surface, she was limp. I cradled her head in my hands, but she wasn't breathing.

"Over here, Shirley!"

Jim was on shore, shouting and waving at me. Blood ran down his face from a cut above his eyebrow. George was at his feet, spinning in tight circles.

I swam on my back, supported Betty's head in my hands and dragged her behind me. When I got close to shore, Jim waded into the pond. He picked her up in his arms and carried her to the beach.

He laid her on the sand and started mouth-to-mouth resuscitation. George stood beside him, watching.

I crawled out of the water and collapsed on the shore. I was exhausted and more frightened than I had ever been in my life.

George waddled over to me and gave my chin a sloppy kiss. I scooped him into my arms, held him close and watched Jim work on Betty.

I mentally prepared myself to take over for him if he got tired. There was no need. In less than a minute, Betty coughed up muddy water, and Jim rolled her onto her side.

Her eyelids fluttered, and she took a quick, sharp breath. A split second later, she vomited more of the filthy water.

"We have to get her to Dr. Thompson right now," Jim said.

I ran to the dam in my bare feet. I grabbed my shoes, loosened the laces and slipped them on. I wadded up my socks and stuffed them in the back pocket on my Bermuda shorts.

Jim was already on the footpath carrying Betty to his truck. George lagged behind him by several yards. He was panting, and his tongue was hanging out the side of his mouth.

When I caught up to George, I picked him up and carried him the rest of the way. I opened the cab of Grandpa's truck, laid him on the seat and slammed the door closed.

"I'll be right back, big guy."

Jim was standing beside his father's truck, and I opened the passenger door for him. He settled Betty onto the seat and tucked George's blanket around her shoulders. Her skin was pale, and her breathing was shallow.

"Stick close behind me, Shirley," he said. "I'm going to be driving pretty fast."

He didn't need to worry about that. If I didn't want to get lost, I wasn't about to let him out of my sight.

Thirty-nine

"Ye gods, young lady," Grandma said. "What were you thinking?"

I pulled the afghan around my shoulders, tucked my feet under me and snuggled into the sofa. Thanks to two cups of hot chocolate, I no longer felt chilled to the bone.

"Now, Marie," Aunt Maude said. "Your granddaughter is a hero."

"Hero?" she said. "She could have drowned out there today."

"But I didn't, Grandma," I said. "I'm just fine."

I reached for my third helping of hot chocolate sitting on the coffee table. I wrapped my hands around the cup and let the rising steam warm my nose.

For a minute or two we sat quietly, watching the fire in the fireplace. George was covered with a beach towel and asleep on his blanket next to the hearth.

"Thank goodness Jimmy was with you to help get Betty to Dr. Thompson's," Grandma said.

I was exhausted and fought to keep my eyes open. I understood Grandma had every right to be angry with me. I just didn't have the energy to go over all the details again.

"I'm sorry I didn't tell you I was leaving the potluck," I said. "I didn't want either of you to worry."

"I'm just grateful you're okay," Aunt Maude said. "Dr. Thompson says my little boy's doing just fine."

Grandma put her feet up on the foot stool and leaned back in Grandpa's leather chair. She grabbed an afghan from the basket beside her and laid it across her legs and bare feet.

"You must promise me, young lady, you will never pull a stunt like that again."

I didn't know how I could possibly make such a promise. Never was a very long time.

"I promise I'll try not to, Grandma."

I looked at Aunt Maude and smiled. She looked right at home in the overstuffed chair. Even though it wasn't quite bedtime, she wore her chenille bathrobe and a pair of mule slippers.

"George really had an adventure today, didn't he?" she said.

"Yes, he did, Aunt Maude."

The little pug rolled onto his side, and the towel slipped off his back. His hair was finally dry thanks to the heat from the fireplace.

"You're such a good boy, George," Aunt Maude said.

At the sound of his name, he lifted his head and looked up at her. I felt the connection between them, and I was so thankful I was able to rescue him.

"I wish I could teach you to swim, big guy," I said.

"That's okay, Shirley," she said. "We'll just keep him away from water from now on."

I chuckled at that. I didn't think she really meant he'd never have another bath. But maybe she did.

"I do have news about Betty," Grandma said to me. "The doctor is keeping a close eye on her."

"Oh?"

"He wants to make certain she doesn't develop pneumonia."

"Okay."

I wished Betty well, but I wasn't interested in her condition at the moment. It was too soon after our ordeal to feel much sympathy, so I changed the subject.

"There must be an awful mess at the café after the potluck," I said.

"Oh, my, yes," Grandma said. "We'll be there very early tomorrow morning to clean it up."

I groaned a little. I wasn't sure I would have the energy for that. Before I could think how to stall the cleanup, there was a knock at the front door.

That was strange. People in Willowdale didn't just drop in on their neighbors unannounced. They called first.

"I wonder who that could be at this late hour."

"You stay there, Grandma," I said. "I'll go find out."

I put my cup on the coffee table and tossed the afghan over the arm of the sofa. I forced my tired muscles to get me to a standing position.

I slipped on my moccasins and shuffled to the entry hall. It took me a while to get there, but I finally opened the door.

Miss Carter stood outside holding a shadow box filled with pressed flowers. She smiled a little and handed it to me.

"This little box doesn't seem adequate," she said. "Betty and I hope you'll accept it, however, as our thank you for helping her today."

Helped her? Is that what they told everyone? I supposed saving her life could be considered help—in an odd sort of way.

Even so, I never expected a thank you from either of them. I certainly never expected a gift.

"You don't need to thank me," I said. "I'm glad everything turned out okay."

I laid the shadow box on the entry table and waited for her to say good-bye. Instead, she continued to stand on the porch and stare at me.

"Is there something else?"

"May I come in?" she said. "I have something extremely important to discuss with your grandmother."

I hesitated for a moment. I wanted to say no, but my mother taught me better manners than that.

"Please, come in, Miss Carter," I said. "Grandma and Aunt Maude are in the living room."

I stepped aside. She walked straight to the living room without a word or a backward glance.

I couldn't imagine what was so important she needed to come to Grandma's house. I closed the door, ignored my sore muscles and hurried to the living room. I didn't want to miss anything she had to say.

"My niece has caused all of you a great deal of concern," she said. "I sincerely hope this incident doesn't jeopardize our sales arrangement."

She sat down on one end of the sofa, and I sat down on the other end. I wanted to wrap the afghan around my shoulders again, but her arm was resting on it.

"Our sales agreement is business," Grandma said. "Your niece's health is personal."

"That is very gracious of you," she said. "Betty won't be a bother to any of you again."

How could that be? It seemed Betty's whole goal in life was to be a bother to everybody.

"Why is that?" I said.

"Once the sales papers are signed," Miss Carter said, "I'm driving Betty back home to Bowling Green. She won't be working for me ever again."

Grandma pulled the afghan off her legs and dropped her feet to the floor. She scooted to the edge of Grandpa's chair.

"I think that is very wise of you," she said.

Aunt Maude didn't say anything. She sat in the overstuffed chair and watched Grandma and Miss Carter talk.

"Is there anything else you would care to discuss before we meet at the bank tomorrow?" Grandma said.

"I can't think of anything at the moment."

Without another word, Miss Carter and I stood up. She followed me to the entry hall, and I opened the door for her.

"Thank you, again, for the shadow box."

She didn't say anything or even look at me. She stepped outside and walked to her car parked in the driveway.

Forty

The bank was beautiful. I loved going there even though I didn't have reasons to go very often.

It had high coffered ceilings with globe lights hanging from the center of each square. The wooden floor was polished to a shine, and the smell of wood polish was everywhere.

The lower half of the walls and the teller cages were paneled in oak wainscoting. Each teller had his own cage and sat nearly hidden behind a wrought-iron window.

From where I sat in the conference room, I could see the entire main floor area. Several desks in the center of the room were lined up opposite the teller cages. Seated at each desk was a woman typing on an Underwood typewriter.

"If I don't become a teacher," I said to myself, "I'm going to work here."

"Did you say something, dear?"

"I was just thinking out loud."

Today was more special than just conducting business at one of the teller windows. Grandma, Aunt Maude, Miss Carter, and I were seated along one side of an oblong-shaped table. Mr. Daily was seated on the other side, facing us. Several sheets of paper were scattered around the table.

"If you would please look at the paperwork in front of you," Mr. Daily said, "we'll begin."

I had never been to such an important meeting, and I didn't know what to expect. I only knew the sale was a family matter, and Grandma wanted me to be there.

Mr. Daily cleared his throat and shuffled through the papers in front of him. He looked around the table at each of us before he spoke.

"Do you understand the arrangements, Miss Carter?" he said.

"I do," she said, "and I agree with every provision in the documents."

"Mrs. Ivey?"

"I read through the paperwork several times," she said. "I find everything acceptable."

"Miss Ellis?"

"I read your papers," Aunt Maude said. "If Marie thinks everything's fine, so do I."

Grandma hadn't told me anything about any provisions, and I didn't know why she told Aunt Maude. I was family, not her.

Mr. Daily offered Miss Carter one of his pens, and she signed the sales agreement with it. She closed the pen, dropped it into her purse and snapped the clasp closed.

Then, Mr. Daily handed Grandma and Aunt Maude each a pen. He waited for them to sign the same copy of the agreement. When they were finished, they handed the pens back to him.

I was totally confused. Aunt Maude wasn't a member of our family. Why did she sign the papers, too?

A woman at one of the desks came into the conference room with a rubber stamp and an ink pad. Once she put her notary public stamp on the paperwork and signed it, the meeting was over.

"I'll have these papers delivered to the county seat immediately," he said. "They should be recorded at the courthouse before the end of the day."

"Thank you, Mr. Daily," Miss Carter said.

She stood up and straightened the wide belt at the waist of her circular skirt. Although she and Grandma were no longer competitors, she was still all business.

"You and I will be speaking very soon, Marie," she said. "We still have numerous personal details to work out."

Before Grandma had a chance to respond, Miss Carter left the room. The sound of her high heels clicking against the wooden floor echoed throughout the building. In a few seconds, the heavy oak door at the front of the bank slammed shut.

"Do either of you have any questions?" Mr. Daily said.

As far as I was concerned, it was too late for questions. Grandma and Aunt Maude already signed the paperwork. There was no longer an Ivey's Café or a farmhouse.

"I can't think of any questions," Grandma said.

Aunt Maude looked at Grandma and said, "I can't either."

Mr. Daily gathered the paperwork and filed it all inside his leather briefcase. He snapped the locks closed and stood up.

"Congratulations," he said. "I hope all your plans are successful."

He shook their hands and walked out the door. Without him there, the room felt empty and oddly quiet.

Neither Grandma nor Aunt Maude seemed upset about selling everything my family had owned for more than three generations. I didn't understand why, and I needed answers.

"Grandma," I said. "What happens now?"

She and Aunt Maude looked at each other. They nodded their heads, and Grandma turned toward me.

"We agree it's time you heard our plans," she said. "After all, they directly affect you."

"I guess they do," I said. "It looks like I'm out of a job and a place to live."

"Just be patient a little longer, dear," she said. "We'll explain it all to you when we meet everyone at the café tomorrow morning."

I didn't have a choice but to wait. It wouldn't do any good to argue or plead my case. I knew Grandma would never change her mind about telling me.

Forty-one

It was a long, restless night for me. I was up and down the stairs several times checking on George.

I hoped Aunt Maude would get up and tell me some details about the sale. I thought I should know something about it before Grandma told everyone else.

It turned out Aunt Maude was as stubborn as Grandma. She went to her room after dinner, and I never saw her again until morning.

After breakfast, we drove to the café, and I carried George into the game room. He spun around three times on top of his bed, plopped down and went back to sleep.

"You stay there, big guy," I said. "I'll check on you after the meeting."

When I walked into the kitchen, Irene was at the stove stirring a pan of hot chocolate. Grandma was searching the cupboards for something, and Aunt Maude was at the sink rinsing out six coffee cups.

"Good morning, Irene." I said.

She barely looked in my direction. Her focus was on the pan in front of her.

"I was just sayin' to your grandma how we're startin' the day off kind of late," she said.

"I was reassuring Irene it wasn't necessary to be concerned about the time," Grandma said.

I didn't want to get in the middle of their discussion. I turned around and watched the glass knob on the percolator. The bubbles were turning a rich brown.

"Aren't you even goin' to let those folks in?"

"Not today, Irene."

Several people stood outside the front door. Others sat on the bench in front of the window. Still others had their faces pressed against the glass, watching us.

Grandma stopped opening and closing cupboards and went to the front of the dining room. She grabbed a scrap piece of paper from under the counter and scribbled a note on it.

She taped the paper to the front window where everyone outside could see it. She even pointed at it.

"We're closed," she shouted at them and walked back to the kitchen.

Since I wasn't being any help to anybody, I went out to the patio. I wanted to make sure everything was picked up after the potluck.

That morning, Pastor Lawrence was thoughtful enough to send the youth choir to do the cleanup for us. They did a good job, and there wasn't anything left for me to do. I was extremely happy about that.

They took the folding tables back to the church and moved the patio furniture back inside the fence. Even the tables and chairs in the café were put back in place.

"Hey, Shirley, is this where we're meeting?"

Jim stepped through the open gate with an armful of folded newspapers. He was dressed in his usual grain-covered clothes and baseball cap. The only thing new was the bandage above his eye.

Mr. Martin followed behind him a few steps. His old felt hat was in his hands.

"Mornin," he said.

"Good morning, Mr. Martin."

"I'll just go put these papers inside," Jim said.

"I don't know what Grandma wants to do with them to-day, Jim," I said. "Just put them out here on one of the tables."

He looked confused, but didn't say a word. He walked to the back of the patio and dropped the papers on the corner table.

Mr. Martin sat down at the table in front of the steps. Jim walked over there and sat down across from him.

"What're we doin' here anyways?" Mr. Martin said.

"Grandma will be out soon, and she'll explain everything."

He grumbled and hooked his hat over the back of the chair next to him. He looked around the patio and tapped his fingers on the table.

I knew exactly how he felt. I was impatient, too. I sat down at the table closest to the fence and waited for the meeting like everyone else.

After a few minutes, the French doors swung open. Grandma held a coffee carafe, Aunt Maude carried a pot of hot chocolate and Irene balanced a tray of empty coffee cups. They walked down the steps and set everything on my table.

"Good morning, Jimmy and Mr. Martin," Grandma said. "Thank you for coming."

"What's this all about?" Jim said.

Aunt Maude ignored his question. She looked at me and nodded.

"Would you serve the drinks, Shirley?"

"I'd be happy to."

I filled each cup with coffee or hot chocolate and handed them out to everyone. When I sat back down, Irene was sitting at the table with me.

"I asked you to meet us here because this is the ideal location to make our announcement," Grandma said.

My hot chocolate smelled wonderful. I was sure it was delicious, but I was too nervous to even take a sip.

"Git on with it, Mrs. Ivey," Mr. Martin said.

Grandma took a drink of coffee and then set her cup down next to mine. She brushed out imaginary wrinkles on the skirt of her dress.

"As of this morning," she said, "Ivey's Café is officially closed."

"What?" Irene said.

"Say that again, Mrs. Ivey."

"It's true, Jimmy," Grandma said. "Miss Carter bought Ivey's Café and the farmhouse. We signed the papers yesterday."

"Ya mean ya sold it all?"

"That's right, Mr. Martin," she said. "In one month, you and Irene will be working for Elaine Carter."

"Ya mean I'm out a job fer a month?"

Grandma stepped up to Mr. Martin's table and sat down on the chair next to him. I could see the concern in her eyes for Grandpa's oldest friend.

"You will still be working," she said, "and you will still be getting paid."

He pulled his rumpled handkerchief from his pants pocket. He wiped it across his forehead and the back of his neck.

"How am I gonna be workin' if the café's closed?"

"Elaine left this morning to take her niece back home," she said. "You will be working for Maude and me for the next four weeks."

"You sold the farmhouse, Grandma," I said. "Where are you going to live?"

"First of all, Elaine is turning the farmhouse into a bed and breakfast," she said. "Her carpenters will work on it while she's away."

"Let me get this straight, Mrs. Ivey," Jim said. "Miss Carter is closing the café for a month while she's in Kentucky."

"That's correct."

"While she's there," he said, "some guys are turning your old house into a—what?"

"It's called a bed and breakfast."

"She says it's popular in the big cities," Aunt Maude said. "People stay a day or two, and you cook them breakfast every morning."

"They have complete access to the house and the yard," Grandma said. "It's as though they are in their own home."

"That sounds creepy to me," I said. "Who wants strangers wandering everywhere?"

"I'm with you," Irene said.

"I saw the remodeling plans," Grandma said. "She's adding a bathroom in each of the three large bedrooms upstairs."

"That's a lot of bathrooms," Jim said.

"It only makes sense each guest should have a private bathroom."

"Yeah, I guess so," he said.

"What about my bedroom?" I said. "Is some stranger going to sleep in there, too?"

"No, dear," she said. "I believe she's turning your room into a lounging area."

I didn't know why that news made me feel better, but it did. I just couldn't figure out where that left Grandma and Aunt Maude.

"You still haven't said where you're going to live, Grandma."

"Luckily for Maude and me, Elaine needed more room to expand her business," Grandma said. "She bought the café and sold her coffee shop to us for a very reasonable price."

"Ya mean ya own yer own store agin?" Mr. Martin said.

"Marie and I both own it," Aunt Maude said. "We're equal partners."

"Well, if that don't beat all," he said.

"We're dividing my big apartment into two small ones," she said. "One for each of us."

"Elaine left us all her books," Grandma said. "We're going to turn the main room into the library I've always wanted."

"What a wonderful idea," I said.

"And I'm never ever going back to Illinois."

That was the best news of all. She belonged in Willowdale.

Aunt Maude walked over to Jim and sat down at his table. She reached out and touched his hand.

"We want you to do the remodeling for us."

"I'd be glad to," Jim said. "It'll be a lot of fun."

"What am I gonna be doin'?" Mr. Martin said.

Grandma stood up and walked to the bottom step. When she turned around, there was a huge smile on her face.

"You have proven to be good with boxes," she said. "We need you to help us pack."

He shook his head and wiped his forehead one more time. He wadded up the hankie and stuffed it back inside his pocket.

"How long do I git?"

"We want everything packed up and out of the house in two weeks," she said. "Once everything is moved, we need your help to organize it all at the general store."

Mr. Martin grumbled. He squirmed a little, but he didn't say a word.

"What then, Grandma?"

"While we're packing, Jimmy can start on our remodel."

"Sounds good to me," he said.

"After we're out of the house, Elaine's carpenters will start on that remodel."

"There's just one thing," Jim said.

"What might that be?"

"Everything depends on what you two want done," he said. "It might take me more than two weeks to finish."

I sat up straighter in my chair. Things were moving too fast for me. It was only a day since Grandma sold her café and her house. I couldn't believe we were talking about moving and remodeling.

"Can't we just slow down and think about this a little longer?" I said.

"I'm afraid we don't have that luxury, dear," Grandma said. "In two weeks, you're driving Maude and me to her brother's house in Illinois."

"I am?"

"It will take two weeks to pack her things and move them back here," she said. "That gives Jimmy the extra time to finish our remodel."

I couldn't believe Grandma would let me drive Grandpa's truck all the way to Illinois. But that was fine with me. I was ready for an adventure.

"What about George?" I said.

"Bill Spencer's going to watch him for me," Aunt Maude said. "He'll take really good care of him."

I gave Jim a sidelong look. I wondered how he felt about his father being in charge of George.

"All this is just fine and dandy," Irene said, "but what about me?"

"Well," Aunt Maude said, "we won't have time to cook while we're packing."

"No, I guess you won't."

"Would you like to be our cook for a month?" Grandma said. "You will live with us at the farmhouse for the next two weeks."

"I can do that," Irene said.

"After that, you will cook at the general store for Jimmy and his crew while we are away."

I could see Irene's mind working. She swung her braid around in front of her and twisted the end with her fingers.

"Don't you worry," she said. "You just tell me what you want me to cook."

"I'll pick you up first thing in the morning and drive you out there," Jim said.

"Are ya fergittin' about me?"

"No, Mr. Martin," he said. "I'll pick you up right after I pick up Irene."

Irene twisted the end of her braid again and leaned against her chair's backrest. There was a grin on her face.

"By the way, Jimmy," Grandma said. "Since I no longer own the café, I won't need you to deliver any more papers."

Forty-two

Two weeks wasn't a lot of time to pack up decades of memories, but we had a deadline. We couldn't miss it.

Grandma and Aunt Maude ran me up and down the stairs every day, hauling countless boxes. It looked as though my grandparents never threw anything away. Not even the smallest knickknack.

Grandma never allowed junk in her house, so everything they kept was top quality. After days of packing what she considered treasures, however, I was ready to haul it all to the dump.

I looked around the kitchen at all the boxes we packed. Soon, there would only be room for a path between the hallway and the back door. I didn't envy Irene having to work around all the clutter.

"How is all of this going to fit into her apartment anyway?" I said to myself.

It would have been worse without Mr. Spencer's help. Grandma allowed him to take a truck load of furniture, dishes and the drapes to an auction. Everything he took was sold.

Other than the boxes stacked in the kitchen, there was only a handful of large items to move. They were Grandma's bedroom furniture, the kitchen table and chairs and Grandpa's chair and stool.

Aunt Maude said someone at the auction spoke for all the furniture in my bedroom. Whoever it was agreed to let me keep it until we moved.

"Where do you suppose I'm going to sleep after the move, George?"

The little pug was on his blanket in the corner of the kitchen. His eyes were open, and he stared at me.

"Maybe I'll throw a blanket and a pillow on one of the sofas in the library," I said. "What do you think?"

He ignored me again, and I couldn't blame him. He didn't have anything to worry about. The remodel included a place in Aunt Maude's new apartment for his bed and his bowls.

"You know, George," I said. "Since I'm out of a job, I guess I'll be going home soon."

I hated to think of that possibility. Working for Grandma in Willowdale had become an important part of my life.

"It's a good thing Grandma and Aunt Maude and Irene are in town right now," I said to him. "I wouldn't be very good company."

I laid a box of Christmas decorations on the kitchen table and walked over to him. My arms and back ached, and I envied the little pug. All he had to do all day was sleep and look cute.

"Do you mind if I sit with you for a minute?"

I collapsed onto the floor and ran my hand down his back. His hair was soft but thin, and his whole face was grey.

"I wish we could stay here forever," I said, "but I know you'll love Aunt Maude's new apartment."

In a few seconds he was asleep again. This time his nose twitched, and he yipped a little. I imagined him dreaming of chasing rabbits or running alongside Jim's bike. Whatever his dream was, I hoped he was having a wonderful time.

My day dreaming was interrupted by the sound of a truck on the gravel driveway. A few seconds later, someone walked up to the back door and knocked.

I looked up and saw Jim at the screen door. His arms were loaded with a stack of old beach towels.

"Hey, Shirley."

"Hi, Jim."

"I brought these back from the general store," he said. "What should I do with them?"

"Are they good or full of holes?"

"They're pretty old."

"Toss them in Grandpa's truck with the rest of the garbage," I said. "I'll haul them to the dump."

For some reason he didn't move. He stood there and stared at me through the door.

"Shirley?"

"Yeah?"

"Could I keep a few of these for rags?"

"Take as many as you want."

"And Shirley?"

"Yeah?"

"Would you mind if I came in and visited with George?"

I was tired and feeling sorry for myself. The last thing I needed was company, but I promised he could visit anytime.

"I guess so," I said. "Come on in."

He dropped the towels on the porch, came inside and pulled his cap off his head. The crew cut stubble was growing out. His new wavy, blond hair looked more like the Jim I knew.

He hung his cap by the back door and plopped down on the floor beside me. He reached over and scratched behind George's ears. The little pug rolled onto his side, stretched his legs and yawned.

"He's sure going to like living in Aunt Maude's general store again," he said.

"Yes, he is."

Jim didn't say anything else for a minute. He was too quiet. I suspected the old towels weren't the only things on his mind.

"Are you going to the square dance at the Grange tonight?" he said.

"Nope."

"Me neither."

Again, we sat without speaking. Did he really drive all the way from town to talk about the dance?

My legs were cramped from sitting too long on the hard floor, but I refused to get up. I didn't want to leave him alone with George.

"Sounds like most everyone in the county will be there," he said.

"That's what I hear."

He looked at me with his blue eyes and his wide, toothy smile. For some reason that made me feel uncomfortable.

"You sure you don't want to go tonight?" he said.

"I'm sure."

"Yeah, me neither."

My legs were killing me, and I jumped up to get the blood flowing again. I was surprised when Jim stood up at the same time and put his hand on my shoulder.

"I hope you'll forgive me someday for being such an idiot about George."

He took his hand away, but I could still feel its warmth. I didn't know why that bothered me, but it did.

"I will," I said. "I just need a little more time."

"Okay," he said. "That's fair."

He looked around the kitchen at all the boxes. He shook his head and walked toward the back door.

"I have to get back to town," he said. "Thanks for the old towels."

When he got to the door, he turned around. He wore that wide, toothy smile again.

"If you change your mind about the dance, let me know."

"I won't change my mind."

He plucked his cap off the hook and put it back on his head. He hesitated for a second and threw me a wave.

"Good-bye, Shirley," he said. "Good-bye, George."

"Wait," I said. "You never did tell me where you got all the lumber and the limestone for Grandma's patio."

"No, I didn't."

Before I could ask him more about them and how much they cost, he walked outside. He let the screen door slam shut behind him.

I stayed beside George while he scooped up the pile of towels. As he ran off the porch, he waved at me one last time.

"Why do you suppose he won't talk about the lumber and the limestone, George?"

There was something strange about it. Before I left for home, I was going to make it my business to find out what it was.

Forty-three

I smelled Grandma's coffee, and I lay in bed enjoying the aroma one last time. It reminded me of every morning I spent in the old farmhouse.

"Well," I said to myself. "This is it."

I got up, changed into my clothes and set my canvas suitcase on the built-in window seat. I emptied the dresser drawers and the closet and packed it all.

After I stripped the linens, I folded and stacked them on the foot of the bed. In the back of the closet, I found the paper grocery bag from last summer. I stuffed everything from the desk inside of it.

With nothing left to do, I closed the suitcase and put it on the floor. I sat down on the seat and looked out the dormer window for the last time.

I was going to miss looking out at Grandma's rose garden and all the beautiful trees. I was even going to miss seeing the water tower in town and the dusty county road.

Thinking about what I would miss made my stomach hurt. It was as if somebody stole a piece of my soul and left a big hole inside of me.

"Come on, Shirley," I said. "You can't let Grandma see you this way."

I got up and scanned the room once more. Tears rolled down my cheeks, and I wiped at them with the back of my hand.

I picked up the suitcase and grocery bag, stood up straight and took a deep breath. Moving to the general store was a new start for Grandma. I wasn't going to spoil it for her.

On my way to the staircase, the hallway felt bare. The only things left on the walls were faded shadows where each picture used to hang.

I took the staircase one step at a time and stopped at the landing to look around. The house echoed with most of the furniture gone and all the drapes off the windows.

Grandma came up behind me and put her arm around my waist. I wanted to be strong for her, so I fought back more tears.

"It's going to be just fine, dear," she said. "Your grandpa would be pleased for Aunt Maude and me."

"Would he really?"

"He knew my dream, and I think he's happy I've decided to follow it."

Grandma always knew the right thing to say. Somehow, I felt better about the move, and my stomach stopped hurting.

"I think I'm getting hungry," I said. "Let's go get something to eat."

She dropped her arm, and I turned to go to the kitchen. Instead of coming with me, she didn't move.

"What is it, Grandma?"

"I was hoping you'd find your appetite."

She dug into the patch pocket on the front of her sundress and pulled out Grandpa's truck keys. She dangled them in front of me.

"You'll need these."

"You want to eat at the café?"

"Oh, no," she said. "Not today."

She dropped the keys into the grocery bag and hurried toward the back of the house. It wasn't easy keeping up with her with the suitcase and grocery bag in my hands.

When we got to the kitchen, Aunt Maude and George stood by the back door. The wicker picnic basket was on the floor beside them.

"What is this, Grandma?"

"Before we leave for Illinois today, we want to do something special to mark the occasion."

"I love picnic breakfasts," I said, "but where's Irene?"

"She went home to do her laundry," Aunt Maude said. "She starts cooking at the general store tomorrow."

I was really going to miss Irene. For two weeks, it was like having an older sister in the house.

"It's getting late," Grandma said. "Shall we go?"

I dropped the suitcase and paper bag on the floor. I threw my arms around Grandma's neck and gave her a huge hug.

I went over to Aunt Maude and put my arms around her frail shoulders. I gave her a gentler hug.

"My gracious," she said. "I sure have missed these hugs of yours."

"Me, too," I said.

I dug the truck keys out of the grocery bag. Then, I picked up the basket and the two blankets on the table. It only took me a minute to load everything in the back of the truck. It took a little longer to squeeze three people and one pug into the cab.

Once we were all settled, I leaned forward and looked around George on Aunt Maude's lap. Grandma sat next to the passenger window with a smug look on her face.

"Where to, Grandma?"

"Just drive, dear," she said. "I'll give you the directions as we go."

Grandma wasn't a driver, and that explained why we turned up and down so many roads. Just when I thought we were lost, she shouted at me.

"Stop the truck!"

Aunt Maude wrapped her arms around George, and Grandma braced her hands against the dashboard. I braked as hard as I could without throwing all of us into the windshield.

When the truck came to a stop, Grandma didn't have to tell me where we were. I recognized the old house immediately. The only thing missing was Mr. Wilson's dog, Sebastian.

"Can you find your way to the pond from here?"

"In my sleep," I said.

I pulled into the driveway and drove through the barnyard and around the dilapidated outbuildings. Behind the last one was the dirt track.

Grandpa's truck was narrower than Mr. Spencer's. Like the last time I was there, I didn't have any problem maneuvering between the fence and the creek.

At the dead end, Mr. Spencer's truck and Pastor Lawrence's car were parked next to each other. I pulled Grandpa's truck alongside the pastor's car and parked close to the birch trees.

"Looks like everybody's here, Marie."

"I hope they aren't getting impatient with us."

"What's going on, Grandma?"

We all climbed out of the truck, and I lowered George to the ground. I had no idea what was happening, and neither of them bothered to explain.

"Come along, dear."

They didn't wait for me to unload the truck. Aunt Maude and George started up the footpath and disappeared among the trees. Grandma followed closely behind them and was out of sight in seconds.

"That's alright," I said to myself. "I don't need any help."

I threw the blankets over my arm, picked up the basket and hurried up the path. It didn't take long to catch up to them.

When we got to the pond, I worried how I would react. I was afraid my ordeal with Betty would cloud my opinion of it. It didn't.

The surrounding woods, the sandy beach and the rippling water were gorgeous. I couldn't help but fall in love with the place.

Jim and Pastor Lawrence were seated on a blanket next to the water. Mr. Martin and Mr. Spencer were in the two folding canvas chairs. Stretched out next to Mr. Martin was a very mellow Sebastian.

"Good morning, everyone," I said.

In unison, they all said, "Good morning."

"You finally got here," Jim said. "We thought you were lost."

I laughed at him, but I didn't take his argument bait. I handed the basket to Grandma and spread both blankets on the sand. Aunt Maude sat down immediately, and Grandma set the basket next to her.

"My granddaughter did a fine job of getting us here."

"Thank you, Grandma."

George slogged through the sand and up to the collie. I moved forward a step. I was ready to do whatever was necessary to rescue him from the guard dog.

I didn't need to worry. George plopped down next to Sebastian and leaned up against him. The collie nuzzled the little pug's neck and licked his ear.

"It's alright, Shirley," Mr. Spencer said. "Those two dogs have been friends a long time."

"I see that," I said.

Mr. Martin tilted his fishing hat away from his face and looked at the picnic basket. He shifted a little and sat up as straight as possible in the sling chair.

"We gonna eat or talk?" he said.

"I guess we're all hungry," Aunt Maude said. "You want to hand out the sandwiches, Marie?"

Grandma opened the picnic basket and began handing a sandwich and an apple to everyone. Before she handed Jim or me our share, Jim stood up and walked over to me.

"There's something I want to show you," he said.

He didn't give me a chance to say anything. He just walked right by me.

"Keep up," he said over his shoulder.

No matter how rude he was, I was too curious not to follow. I turned on my heel and practically ran to keep up with his pace.

"Don't be long, you two," Grandma called after us. "We have to be on our way soon."

Jim led me away from the pond and the sandy beach to a meadow just beyond the birch trees. He stomped out a path in the tall grass for me to follow.

At the back of the meadow was a windbreak of ancient cottonwood trees and a low, wire fence. He pushed the top wire down and held it so I could step over.

On the other side was a fallow field that seemed to stretch forever over a series of rolling hills. There were scattered bits of corn stubble poking through the rich black soil.

"Where are we going, Jim?"

"We're almost there."

We walked along the perimeter of the field until we found a break in another fence. Jim led me through the break to a level strip of land surrounded by shade trees.

"We're here," he said.

I didn't understand what we were doing there. Finally, he pointed to a pile of rocks a few feet away.

"You wanted to know where all the building materials came from," he said. "This is it."

I walked over to the pile of rocks and realized it wasn't a pile of rocks at all. It was a stack of limestone.

Beyond the limestone were several stacks of lumber in different widths and lengths. Some of the boards were new, but some were extremely weathered. Every stack rested on a series of concrete blocks, keeping it off the ground.

"I started squirreling all of this away when I was twelve," he said.

My mouth dropped open. It was hard to imagine the time and work it took to build such a stockpile.

"Wow, Jim."

"When you designed the patio for your grandma, it was the perfect chance to use some it."

"How did Grandma ever manage to pay for it?"

"That, Shirley," he said, "is between your grandma and me."

I really wanted to know details, but I knew better than to pry. He was a private person, and I respected that.

"Can I ask why you started saving all of this in the first place?"

Jim looked down and kicked at the ground with the toe of his tennis shoe. When he looked up again, his expression was more serious than I had ever seen him wear.

"Dad bought forty acres of Mr. Wilson's farm years ago," he said. "Long before he bought the old mill."

"I hope that includes the pond."

"It does," he said. "Someday, Dad wants me to build a house for him out here."

I was truly impressed and awed by his plans. My plan to be a teacher seemed small and insignificant in comparison.

"That's why you want to be an engineer?"

"No," he said. "That's why I used to want to be an engineer."

"What?"

"After the patio project, I started thinking about changing my major," he said. "When I started work on the general store's remodel, I decided for sure."

I was stunned, and my knees felt a little wobbly. I sat down on the end of a stack of two-by-fours.

"You don't want to be an engineer anymore?"

"Nope," he said. "I'm going to be an architect instead."

"Wow."

He pulled his baseball cap from his head and slapped it against his pant leg. Dust and bits of chaff flew everywhere. The cut above his eyebrow was almost completely healed.

"By the time you get back with Aunt Maude's things," he said, "the general store will be ready to move into."

"I can hardly wait to see it."

He put his cap back on, walked over to the stack of two-by-fours and stood in front of me. His face was relaxed again, and he wore that wide, toothy smile of his.

"Let's go get something to eat," he said. "I'm starved."

When he held his hand out to me, I didn't hesitate for a second. I stood up, slipped my hand into his and walked back to the pond with him, hand in hand.

About the Author

Born in Indiana, Carla J. Underwood grew up in a small town in the northwest corner of the state. She learned both the challenges and the rewards of living in a small community.

She embraced the small-town ideals and opted for a small, out-of-state university. She earned her B.A. degree in Speech Pathology and Audiology.

She and her husband now live in a small town in the desert Southwest. They share their home with their ten-year-old pug.

More about the first two books in the Willowdale, Indiana stories trilogy– *Mrs. Ivey's Café* and *A Dog's Life* –is found at www.mudpiespress.com.